NO
Direction
HOME

A Novel

By

H. A. Maxson

Acknowledgement

The majority of Chapter 2 appeared as a freestanding short story entitled "A Call Late Night" in *Broken Cord: An Anthology of Writing about Alzheimer's and Dementia,* Edited by Hank Kalet, Two Dogs Press, Kendall Park, NJ, 2020. 39-47.

Photo Credits

Cover and Author photos: Maureen Maxson

Published by BLAST PRESS

324B Matawan Avenue

Cliffwood, NJ 07721

(732) 970-8409

gregglory.com

Dedication

For my Wife, Maureen

For my Daughter, Carrie

In memory of my Brother, Wesley S. Maxson 1959-2009

In memory of my Mother, Cathaleen G. Maxson 1926-2010

In memory of my Father, Harry A. Maxson, Sr. 1922-2014

CONTENTS

January 15, 2014

The office was austere. The white sheetrock walls wore no photographs of family or friends, no vacation moments, no expensive paintings or even cheap assembly-line acrylics purchased at a starving-artist sale at the local Weekender Motel. Nothing. In a far corner was a stack of frames that may have held diplomas or may have been empty holes awaiting documents or art, a raison d'etre.

I sat with my wife, Caitlin, and my grown son, Jon. It was only the third time any of us had hunkered down between these walls. Caitlin rummaged through her pocketbook, Jon studied the blank walls as if there might be an exam. My own hands unconsciously tee-peed in a gesture of prayer even though I have avoided any species of services for decades.

We didn't speak. We fidgeted in our own habitual ways. I remember it was quiet, funeral-home quiet. Each of us waited without fuss or bother for Dr. Samuelson. Occasionally the walls ticked, one of us coughed, or a car rolled past on the street outside.

Only once my wife's eyes and mine met—for just one nervous second, then broke. She returned to rearranging her stuff and I to building an Indian village with my hands. Although we said nothing out loud, I suspect each of us, in our own way, expected to hear some variation on doom, some proclamation of hopelessness, some hollow apology for a personal and collective inability to cure, or at least ameliorate, my father's dis-ease.

We sat. Silent. I wanted to puke.

*

The last time we met in this space there had been more of us. My mother was there. My father was there with my sister holding his hand and trying to calm his impatience. I spent my time then, too, looking around at the near emptiness and randomness and thinking it looked more like a freshman dorm room piled with new stuff from Wal Mart and old, familiar things to blunt the shock of moving into a new life.

I remember looking at the books on the slightly sloping shelves. Some lay on their sides. Some leaned as if returned by someone preoccupied or indifferent. I remember thinking cattywumpus, wonkerjawed. I remember being thankful for those fifty or sixty books jumbled like so many mimes practicing casual poses.

Dr. Samuelson entered. A tall, thin, nervous man, he seemed as if he'd rather be anywhere else. What little smile he managed was unnatural, as if his secretary had just reminded him to loosen up. He didn't want to, and he wasn't quite sure how. Like his books, he was there, frankly, because he had to be.

"Folks," he said, as much observation as greeting, sitting behind his gray metal desk, a refugee, no doubt, from a salvage store. "You've seen the change in your father, umm, husband." He looked at Jon for a moment, then shrugged, choosing, I suppose, not to add to his list. Looking at my father, he nodded ever so slightly. Dad didn't notice. He would have stood up and walked out had my sister, Bonnie, not anchored him and patted down his urge to run.

The doctor sat board straight. His eyes made a circuit of our faces. "There is no sugarcoating this, and there is no more doubt in my mind—Warren has Alzheimer's disease. There are some promising drugs, but they only delay the symptoms, slow down the inevitable. There is no cure, as you already know." He collapsed slowly backward into the dilapidated oak office chair. He looked down at his hands lying on the desk as if his short speech had exhausted and defeated him. I was thankful the apologies I expected didn't follow. I distain apologies for things people have no control over.

We didn't speak, having expected as much, or worse. My mother began to cry and looked at me as if I might contradict the doctor's diagnosis as preposterous or impossible. I shook my head, there being nothing else to do. Caitlin went to my mother's side and hugged her. God bless wives and sisters.

As if we had rehearsed the moment, we all exhaled and each of us searched for a neutral place where we could safely rest our eyes with nothing more challenging than books and cobwebs to consider.

Without warning or another word, the doctor unfolded himself from the chair and the moment and left that white, quiet space.

My very earliest memory—I was maybe two or three years old— takes place in Ocean County Park on a Sunday afternoon. That memory is not long or complicated or particularly vivid, it's kind of foggy actually. It is merely old. I am sitting on a blanket with my father. We are on a large open lawn surrounded by tall pine trees. The grass is very green, and my father is in shirt sleeves. I don't know what we were doing other than sitting in the sun. A hill, also grassy, ran up in front of us. I would like to say the rest of the family is on top of the hill, but I don't know that.

The action is simple. My father and I spot a gray squirrel crossing the wide lawn. He was cautious so there must have been other people around (pure speculation). He would take three or four steps. Stop. Sit up and look around. He did this all the way across the lawn. Hop. Hop. Hop. Sit up. Rotate his head.

My father motioned for me to lie down, as he had done, facing the squirrel. We lay very still and quiet and watched the animal very closely. He had something, an acorn or small pine cone, in his paws. Nothing, no dog or small child threatened him, but he remained very aware all the way across the open space until he could scamper up one of the pine trees.

At some point many years later it occurred to me that this was probably the first time I deliberately observed something just for the pure pleasure of it. Lying still and watching might have served me very well as a hunter had I chosen to kill things, which I did not. I had no model for that. I came from observers and growers, not hunters.

Nathan Samuelson looked younger than his years. He was young, just not as young as his shaggy hair and five o'clock shadow made him out to be. Simple math said he couldn't be *that* young. But we had the impression that in twenty or thirty years he would stumble and falter when he had to tell families a senior member of the clan was sick or dying. He probably should have gone into research—which he had— and stayed away from practice—which he hadn't—so now we fidgeted and rearranged and gazed off while we awaited the announcement that brought the remaining members of our tribe together—namely Caitlin, Jon and me—in his shambling office, books askance, cobwebs ever increasing, to await…what? Once a death sentence has been announced, what then?

Myself, I'm an academic, have been since Hector was a pup, many decades. Caitlin is a nurse, has been forever. Usually I sit on the other side of the desk from an undergrad who fails to comprehend that in college four D's and two F's add up to a failing grade, not one more narrow escape, that a D is no longer a "skin of my teeth" escape from the gallows. Here it is, "Do not pass Go. Do not collect two hundred dollars," or whatever the equivalent is on the updated board. I don't know Samuelson's discomfort. I usually face a black and white situation, though his might be if we exchange black and white for life and death. We knew Dad was dying. Not tomorrow or next week or even next year, but the prognosis was fixed.

When he entered the nursing home in late 2009—against his written wishes—he ate solid food, told stories that still transfixed an audience, cared, pretty much, for himself, and held conversations that clung together, admittedly, with spit and a prayer. We followed familiar narrative arcs out of habit. Even when he snuck in unfamiliar details and nuances, we barely blinked or noticed. We heard, even when we didn't hear, the same old, same old. Over the years he told us more and more, but, most of us did not fill in the blanks. What we heard were the set pieces we knew by heart, what we missed/ignored were the tiny fragments he added over the years in increments we grew accustomed to ignoring. The autobiography we thought we knew grew, changed, was decades in the process of becoming—and he built it around us unawares.

In that way, and perhaps in that way only, the two men who summoned us to this office were alike. One had a story to tell that was lost, the other had a tale to tell of what might be, not the familiar what had been. Was, is, might be sat in an office, books on shelves suggesting modern dance positions. Blank sheet rocked walls awaiting pen or brush or spatter of paint.

We were there and suddenly he was there with us, his face giving nothing away. He unfolded himself into the old scarred chair. No expression when he looked at us. A small smile, but perhaps I willed it or imagined it.

"Folks," he began as he had five years before.

I sighed. I watched my wife and son adjust themselves in the folding chairs.

"I have some news."

"Good? Bad?" one of us asked.

"You decide," he said.

And we let that settle like a sheet over a bed. It drifted down slowly.

"We decide? How does that work?"

I don't think it was art at work in the silence that followed a bit too long. I believe he genuinely did not know how to respond. The smile was a facial tick, the hesitation a moment to bring together a piece of information fraught with complication and subtleties never imagined before.

We let it hang in the air.

"There appears to be—a cure. A number of Alzheimer's patients have been brought back, so to speak, returned to full cognition." He went quiet.

We did the same. *Dad. Back?*

Before we could respond the doctor pulled his vanishing act again. We waited quietly for several minutes thinking he would return for our reaction. He did not. Now accustomed to the silence of that unholy space, and the three of us once again fascinated with our own hands, or scuffed paint on the floor in front of us, we continued to sit. Of course, I can only speak of my own thoughts, but they were a sleigh ride over bumpy ground. Just when I thought I'd reached a smooth stretch of snow, I hit a mogul and spun off into strange and unfamiliar territory.

Judging by their silences, Jon and Caitlin were both careening down the same slope.

I broke the silence with a cough. "I suppose he expects us to see ourselves out," Caitlin offered.

"I suppose so," I said. Jon nodded and stood up.

We didn't discuss what we had just been told. We didn't even mention it. I don't know if we just needed time to digest what we had been told or whether alone and together we were uncertain if we had actually heard what we thought we heard. I knew that experiments had been conducted over the years—and failed. Others had had a modicum of success. My father, through my mother and I acting as proxies, had been invited several years before to join a study testing a drug that had successfully returned seven out of ten trial participants to full or nearly full memory, all symptoms vanished. My mother was one hundred percent in favor of enrolling him immediately. I chose to mull it over, then discuss it with my sister and Caitlin. My mother was furious, and I almost abandoned my caution. But I held out another week.

And in that week something awful began to happen. One by one patients who had shown a nearly miraculous recovery of speech, mobility, clarity of thought, and most of all, memory, began to lapse back into the fog and darkness they had inhabited for so long. I once heard this state described as being like waking up every day in a city you did not know and whose local language you did not speak. Some doctors involved in the study speculated that the sudden collapse back into silence and confusion was worse because of the speed of the decline. What had taken years to realize now took only a few days, and in a few cases only hours. For most of the patients in the trial their disease was like the proverbial frog in the soup pot. Symptoms developed over many years, sometimes decades, so that changes were slowly assimilated into what was a new reality. Even the patients grew to accept the grasping for words, names, yesterday's dinner items as the way it had always been. Not so this time. Unknown to them and their families, this recovered lucidity and its attending joy came with a horrifyingly short shelf life, not a shining future. Because the relapse was so quick they saw or felt the change coming over them, and according to some reports from wives and husbands and children, each of the patients was terrified of the crash they saw coming and were helpless to avoid or even understand it.

As I followed the story on-line and in the newspapers I bought on my way to the nursing home, I shared it with only Caitlin and Jon. By then my mother was weakening from her years-long fight against cancer that had metastasized to the big bones. What strength she had left went into worrying about herself and trying to hang on despite the fact that the pain had outflanked the chemo and the handfuls of pills she clung to like a religion. She found a little comfort in knowing my father was cared for in the next wing of the nursing home. But he may as well have been on the other coast.

I spent my days, three or four of them each week, hiking back and forth between the North wing and the South wing, visiting one while the other napped or ate. But that arrangement couldn't last. As soon as the Fall semester began, my visits would be curtailed, consigned to weekends, Tuesdays and Thursdays, and, of course, holidays. About that time some well-meaning someone suggested that I look for the light at the end of the tunnel. And I found it. Unfortunately, it was the headlight on a locomotive.

June 2009

I had always heard, and personally knew to be true, that it was never good when the phone rang in the middle of the night. At a time when my mother had undergone several open-heart surgeries over three or four years, and only then was diagnosed with the cancer that had metastasized, and my father could still recall where he'd served and what he'd done over five decades before as a sergeant in the U.S. Army, but couldn't remember what day of the week it was, the phone rang, first at my parents' house, then at mine.

My father answered, I later learned, but couldn't understand what the voice was telling him. He hung up and went back to bed. The police officer then called me.

"Mr. Wilson, I'm sorry to be calling so late. I tried talking to your father, but he hung up on me."

"He has dementia, Alzheimer's."

"I'm sorry."

"Thank you. What is this about?"

"Your sister has been in a serious automobile accident."

"Jesus Christ."

"I think you should come to Mercy General right away."

"I'll dress and come over," I told him, "thanks for understanding about my father."

"Yes, sir. I'm sorry about your sister. Sounds like you've got your hands full of problems."

"You don't know the half of it."

By that time Caitlin was awake and trying to read my face. "What is it?" she asked the moment I hung up.

"Bonnie's been in a car accident. I don't know the details, but it's serious. She's at Mercy."

"I'll let Jon know we're going, then I'll get dressed. Do you want coffee?"

"No." I looked at the clock for the first time. It was 2:43. I blinked the last chimera of a dream from my head and stood up. Caitlin handed me the phone.

"Will aunt Bonnie be ok?" he asked with a shaky voice. My sister and my son were very close.

"I don't know, buddy. The officer who called just said there's been an accident."

"Should I meet you there?"

"No, you've got to go to work."

"Yeah, like I'd be able to concentrate."

I was rummaging in my sock drawer. "Listen," I told him, "do what you feel is best."

"I'll see you there."

Caitlin and I dressed quickly. "Jon will meet us," I told her. I don't remember the ride.

*

We drove directly to the emergency room. Every overhead light was on. At 4:30 a.m. it might as well have been noon. Some white coats hustled, others dawdled writing in charts or talking to patients' family members. All of the nurses, in scrubs, seemed like they were in a controlled, perpetual chaos. We identified ourselves and were shown to the curtained room behind which my sister lay. If I hadn't been told, I would not have recognized my sister. Her face was swollen and bruised. Tubes and wires were a spider's web in which she was trapped. I put my arm around Caitlin's shoulder, the other around Jon's. For a moment I allowed myself to ask, How much more? What else can we take?

"She should recover," a nurse offered in passing. It was meant as a kindness, an encouragement, but at the moment it seemed gratuitous. I nodded a curt thank you.

At times like that anyone not wearing white or scrubs feels helpless—and maybe some of them do too. I can only imagine. After a short while, with no one else offering a diagnosis, prognosis or sympathy, we drifted to a kind of waiting area with year-old magazines and a television mutely selling some product to a mostly sleeping world.

About five o'clock I asked Jon if he would pick up his grandparents. "I'll call and explain what's going on. They should be ready when you get there."

After Jon left, a young intern came into the otherwise empty room and sat across from us. "Mr. and Mrs. Wilson?"

"Yes," we looked up at him.

"I'm Doctor Whitney. I've been following your sister's case throughout the night. Her injuries seem to be mainly external, hence the bruising and swelling. She was hit pretty hard according to the report I saw a couple of hours ago. We have not, so far, detected any internal bleeding. If there is none, then we are probably looking at a long but full recovery."

I wanted to sigh but thought better of it. Too many "so fars" and "probablies" still hanging in the air. "When will we know?" Caitlin asked him, foregoing the Doctor or even glancing at his name tag.

"Well, I can't say for sure. Maybe as soon as later today, but maybe not for a couple of days. Stay close but don't feel married to the ER."

"We will," I told him. "Thanks for taking the time to fill us in." I expected him to come back with a "my pleasure" or "it's my job." But he didn't. He rose, bowed almost imperceptibly and left the room. Caitlin and I looked at each other but said nothing.

Around seven a.m. Jon lead my parents into the waiting room. The infomercials had given way to news delivered by bright-eyed talking heads whose freshness of voice and hair and costume seemed to mock our fatigue.

Mom knew exactly where she was and seemed to shrink back from every piece of institutional furniture and every glimpse of scrubs and white coats. I stood up and put my arm around her shoulder. Dad was dazed and frightened. Here was a man who, only a few years before, after one of my mother's by-pass surgeries, had stood shoulder to shoulder with me as we drank morning coffee and looked out over the river as sailboats skimmed over small waves and tufts of spume. It reminded him, he told me, of his days crabbing with his uncle on the back bays along the Jersey coast. I'd thought it odd he'd said crabbing instead of clamming but wrote it off to lost sleep and weeks and months of worry. Now he stood, a full head shorter than me, an old man shrunken into nervous confusion.

"How is Bonnie?" my mother asked Caitlin.

"I have to guess that there's been no change. It's been hours since the intern spoke with us."

"Oh, God," she muttered and clung to Jon as if she might faint. Her face was drawn and sallow. She had lost so much weight over the past year that her body's revolt against her health showed in her face, her hands, her posture. She was defeated but refused to surrender. Dad helped her into a chair. We didn't even pretend to care about the news. I was pretty sure everyone shared my wish for a little sleep and a lot of escape.

Dr. Whitney returned a little while later looking haggard and worse for wear. He sat heavily, elbows on knees, eyes on the floor between his shoes. I introduced him to my parents. He gave them a nod, then sighed. He seemed surprised to see us all looking at him, waiting.

"The bruising. The swelling. We thought that was the extent of her injuries."

"They're not?"

"No," he said, looking to each of us. "We've found a small bleed."

"Where?" Jon asked him.

"It's a subarachnoid hemorrhage. In the brain." My mother gasped and grabbed for my father's hand. Instinct or habit took over and sixty plus years of marriage told him what to do. He took her hand in both of his. His face was a study of fear and confusion, but he whispered to her, "Better days, better days, hon." To this day I don't know what well he drew that from.

"Is there anything you can do for Aunt Bonnie?" Jon asked the doctor who was younger than himself.

"Drugs, for clotting," he said. "I'll talk to my boss when he gets here. Maybe an hour." He stood up and edged toward the door. "Maybe you all should get some coffee and breakfast." Caitlin told me later she thought he was going to cry. At the door he turned back and looked directly at my mother. "I'm sorry," he said.

"Damnit."

About noon activity around Bonnie's "room" had calmed. A nurse told us a private room would be available within the hour. Caitlin and I convinced Jon and my parents that we should at least try to stomach some food. There was a coffee shop around the corner, so we hiked the half block there and found a booth.

"What'll it be?" I asked, pretending calm and confidence. Truth be told, my stomach was an outsized muscle cramp and it would take a great effort to get even soup down my throat.

Mom had stopped eating beyond subsistence portions of fruit and salad in the past few years. Dad stared at the menu drawing a blank. "What do I like?" he asked my mother. "You choose for me. You always liked to do that." She didn't. Never had. She ordered him a BLT and his life blood, coffee. Only after much coaxing by Caitlin and Jon did she add a fruit cup for herself. We ordered what seemed likely to slide down the easiest—chicken soup and toast for me. I couldn't shake the image of my sister caught up like some innocent insect in the web of tubes.

Brunch was a bust. We wandered back to the hospital hoping to find Bonnie safely relocated to a real room. But ER activity was chaotic both inside and outside her curtain. Dr. Whitney pointed to us and an older doctor hurried our way.

I panicked, "What's going on?" I asked, my voice a pitch higher than normal.

"The small bleed Dr. Whitney told you about this morning has increased. There is a great deal of pressure building up in her cranium from all the blood."

"Can you stop it?" Caitlin asked, a skosh more composed than I was.

"A surgeon has been called. He'll probably order an MRI, maybe a CT scan so he can get a look inside."

"Oh my God," my mother whispered.

"I'll let you know as soon as I have some news." We returned to the waiting room where morning news had given way to soap operas. No one spoke for the next hour.

The neurosurgeon came in around 2:30. Dad was dozing. Mom's hands fretted a Kleenex to tatters. Jon, Caitlin and I pretended to watch the television, but turned our attention to Dr. Horn as soon as he walked into the room. We had not met before and only guessed at who he was. He introduced himself then half sat on the arm of a chair. He was hang dog and looked world weary. Even his scrubs seemed shop worn, though they were clean and, yes, pressed.

We waited, shifted in our seats. Waited. "The bleed in Bonnie's brain is worse than we thought. Much worse. We..." he paused.

"What are the options?" I spoke up when no one else seemed able to.

"Two," he said, then paused as if trying to conjure a third. "Only two."

Another round of squirming.

"Okay," he finally said, "there is no way to soft sell any of this. If I perform surgery to relieve the pressure, she might not survive the surgery."

"Option two?" Jon asked.

"Option two we do nothing and hope the bleeding stops and she recovers. But if she does recover, she may well remain," he paused, "remain in a vegetative state."

"Forever?"

"Very likely, yes."

I swallowed down the lump in my throat. "Not much in the way of options," I said, thinking out loud.

"That's it?" asked Jon standing and reddening with anger. "Two really shitty options? Where in the hell is modern medicine when *we* need it?" He slammed out of the room.

"They are very close," I explained. The surgeon just put both palms toward me. I shut up.

"Not what I signed on for, I can assure you. Save the world and all that. He stood a moment and looked into each of our faces. "I'm sorry." And I knew he meant it. "I'll wait for your decision."

Once again, we were quiet. Mom dabbed at her eyes with the remains of her tissue and for all the world looked like an adult child whose eyes begged us to tell her what to do. Jon returned. He shook his head but did not apologize. I didn't expect him to.

At times of great stress, like this one, time does very weird things, contracts or dilates, minutes become hours, or seconds. I could not gauge how much time had passed as we each swam deep into our own thoughts, memories, especially those in which Bonnie played a big part.

At some point in the foggy block of time Dr. Horn returned to the room. His face had aged another decade. "There was no time. No time left. I'm sorry, Bonnie died at 4:03 of a massive stroke."

Mom and Caitlin held each other and cried. Dad had at some point woken from his nap and now stared at his wife and daughter-in-law holding each other together. He frowned at me. Jon put a hand on his shoulder, then whispered in my father's ear. His expression was hard to read.

A nurse came in in a few minutes to see if we needed anything. Looking at my father, she caught the vague expression on his face. She knelt beside him. Mr. Wilson, do you understand what's happened?"

He sat still for a moment, then looked at her. "My child just died."

As a boy, I spent a lot of time in Bayside Cemetery. My grandfather was the caretaker and had been since the Depression. My father dug graves to earn extra money, five dollars per grave. I remember sitting on the hood of my father's car, headlights trained across the gravesite as my father laid out the two by twelves that defined the shape of the grave. Jewish graves had to be dug, and the body buried, before sunrise. So, he would dig through the night and then go to work at six a.m. Rare, but it happened.

At five or six or seven years old my father took me with him on those night time digs. As he dug he talked about his softball team and his bowling team—both of which were named the Boondockers. And through the night he would disappear into the ground. First legs, then body, then his head sank until all that was left was his voice rising through the red clay, from the sand four feet down. Here, about half the time, the hole collapsed burying my father to the waist.

Hour after hour I listened to stories, then curses when the sand caved in and he had to spend another hour digging himself free. Every few minutes, the top of his head now level with the ground, he would ask, "are you still there?"

"I am." I would sing back, intent on watching the sand fly up and over the wooden framework of the grave. All night I listened to crickets, cicadas and my father sinking ever deeper into the earth.

To this day I do not whistle past any graveyard.

Summer 2006

Sometime in 2006 my parents had gone shopping at Shop Rite about ten miles from home. Despite her diminished physical resources, Mom went off to grocery shop while Dad sat on a bench in the front of the store, hoping, I guess, for someone, anyone, to join him and engage in conversation. By that time, he never left the house without his WWII baseball cap on his head adorned with miniature versions of his war-time medals and ribbons. He genuinely relished being saluted by younger men and thanked for his service.

Although he rarely talked about his time in the Army--his stint in the Philippines at the peak of the War--when I was young, but he bent every conversation to the War after he hit about age 85. We all marveled at how deftly he could manipulate someone's comment about a swimming pool to a general conversation about water and then to his experience aboard a troop ship headed for the Southwest Pacific during a typhoon. Ten thousand gallons of chlorinated fresh water were alchemized into the salt water of the Pacific Ocean without the conversant ever noticing the slight-of-voice until well after the conversion. Masterful.

As family we had heard every story dozens, if not hundreds, of times. So, we smiled, nodded and tuned him out. But a new, unsuspecting bench-mate never knew what hit them. One minute they were swapping chit chat and social noise, the next they were at Clark Field in Manila, or standing on Rizal Avenue facing shop windows to avoid having to salute General MacArthur. They were whiplash inducing leaps through time and space, and Dad was the admiral of the time machine that shot you from here to there in so few sentences it was scary. And the amazing thing was his audience, gathered from the bench by a wife, always left after shaking his hand, with a smile and a "glad to have met you." He was the very definition of raconteur.

Apparently on this day no one sat next to him and he grew bored or restless or both, and he left. He forgot my mother, wandered into the parking lot, found his car and drove away. When my mother returned to the bench after checking out, the bench was empty. Seeing her distress, an employee asked if she needed help. She explained the situation, and several employees fanned out across the store. No old man wearing a baseball cap with WWII military paraphernalia on it was found. My mother sat and cried.

Meanwhile, Dad realized he was lost smack dab in the middle of the township he had once represented as a county commissioner. He could talk your ear off about 1944 but could not GPS himself within the few square miles he's lived in for eight decades. By design or dumb luck, he eventually found the police station, went inside and reported that he was lost. After running his license plate, they drove him home.

A Shop Rite employee drove my mother.

"Hi," he said when she arrived home. "Where have you been?" She told me later that she fixed him with a look that sixty-odd years of marriage had sharpened to a lethal point. She didn't speak to him for two days.

After that adventure, my mother took over the driving duties, only slightly the lesser of two bad options.

February 2014

I had taken Dr. Samuelson's information and tossed it into my subconscious like a grain of sand into an oyster hoping it would irritate an answer to a pearly brilliance. My day to day brain worked overtime to suppress what screamed to be considered and discussed with Caitlin and Jon. And some days that worked well enough for a few hours, even a whole waking day. But the nights, I could not control the dreams. I have a stock of dream images—water, old houses, ruined woods and rooms—that I've come to respect over the years and expect to show up when particular stresses and situations arise. But I never could have imagined the new set of images my unconscious concocted in the days following our visit with Dr. Samuelson at the nursing home. Just as old cartographers came to label unknown or unexplored places with tags like "There be Monsters," or "There be dragons," I came to see my dreamscapes as terrifying places where the unthinkable might happen to my father if he was allowed access to the newest experiment designed to save him.

Within a few days I realized our entire family had become disagreeably quiet and moody. We were civil to one another. Period. We went to work, cooked meals, cleaned the house—Jon his apartment—and performed the rest of our quotidian domestic drudgeries with as little comment and conversation as possible. Later, Caitlin confided that she wondered how long the silence could go on, how long before the dam holding back our individual and collective frustrations and uncertainties, not to mention potential joy, would burst and we as a family drown in rage and sorrow.

Alzheimer's keeps you in a constant state of anger—not the patient, they are beyond the anger—but the family, from the oldest to the youngest, and it takes a toll. Eventually I permitted myself to think back about former trials, ones we had fortunately come too late for, or delayed long enough to discover the heartache heaped on the participants whose salvation was short-lived and who had shrunk back into fog, all the while watching themselves disappear. I wouldn't allow that, yet another insult to my father's dignity. Let's wait, I thought. It's like the first year of a new car model. It's bright and shiny and nobody else has one. First on the block and all that. But then no one's yet broken down on a cold night on a dark road without cell reception in their new-mobile. Let's wait.

"It'll make your head spin" is a metaphor for indecision, I get it. But when you set yourself up with just two decisions (yet multiple possible outcomes due to each decision) you are like a runner in a game of one-a-cat, or a hitter caught in a run-down between second and third. Some days my head spun like a screwball.

My wife is not by nature moody, but in the days following our visit to Samuelson's office, she was downright taciturn. I wondered if she were just giving me space to think, or if she too fought the battle of the diad like I did. Together we might have been stronger and smarter, but we're both the oldest child in our families. We chose to face the dragons alone.

Jon was the first to breech the self-imposed silence we'd condemned our house and family to. "So," he began after the salad and before the pot roast, "have you given any thought to the good doctor's news about the latest Alzheimer's breakthrough?"

That pebble rippled our silence.

"I haven't thought about much else, Jon, if you allow my letting that roulette-ball of an idea to bounce around my subconscious one sixty-eight. If you mean am I ready to sit down with you and your mother to make a decision, then no, no I'm not. Caitlin?" I glanced at her across the table, she was masticating a tiny crust of bread and looked very serious about what she was about to share.

"Yes, I have. My subconscious has also been giving the idea a workout, but I've also spent time consciously weighing Dr. Samuelson's words. So far all of the promising drugs, the therapies and surgical invasions have proven to be chimeras, cats line dancing."

"What?" said Jon with a smile.

"You know," I said, "photo-shopped fantasies. We want to believe so badly we exaggerate any appearance of a phenomenon. Cats line dancing! If you let a camera run long enough you'll eventually film something extraordinary, like what seems to be a choreographed move."

"Then your mind plays it over and over on a loop. You want it to be true, so your mind convinces you it is." Caitlin finished my rough explanation.

"Like that movie with Robin Williams where he plays a neurologist whose patients awaken from comas?"

"*Awakenings*," Caitlin and I said simultaneously. "And yeah, something like that, and in the end they all went back into their comas," I said.

"We've seen that plot when it was not on a movie screen. It was awful to watch," Caitlin added.

"But if we wait until science can one hundred percent assure us that Grandpa will recover, he might be dead for years."

"True," I said, "but we also don't want to kill him before his time."

"Right, Dad, but didn't you tell me when I was a kid that Grandpa had made you swear that if he ever lost his mind that you would kill him? Didn't he tell you that wasn't living, it was only existing, and he wanted no part of it?"

"Just like he didn't want any part of a nursing home either, but he and Grandma couldn't live alone any longer, they'd have hurt themselves or each other. Trust me, it's not easy going against your parent's wishes," I said.

"They don't cover any of this in the handbook," Caitlin added.

"What handbook?" Jon snapped.

"Exactly," his mother said.

Sometime in the late fifties, on a rare night off, my father needed to get the car inspected. The inspection station was ten or fifteen miles away. He told me that when we were done we'd stop at Carvel for an ice cream cone. I would have been happy to go without the enticement. Such outings were rare.

At the inspection station they failed the car because a headlight was burned out. We took it around the corner to a filling station where they changed out the light. Back at the inspection station the car passed, and they slapped an inspection sticker on the lower right corner of the windshield. Once we pulled out of the station, noisy with horns, screeching brakes and windshield wipers, he stopped the car. "I'm sorry," he said to me.

"For what?" I asked, truly puzzled.

"I don't have any money left for ice cream."

"I don't care, Daddy." Years later, in grad school, I remembered this incident and wrote my father a letter asking him if he remembered. I don't remember if he did or not. But at the end of the letter I wrote, "That was the best damned ice cream I ever ate."

August 2009

For about a year before my mother died I took Dad to his medical appointments and med adjustments every other Thursday. Because he saw him only every other week, and I saw him all of the time, Dr. Alford always spotted areas where Dad had lost ground—if not the moment we walked into the office, then the instant my father spoke.

My father was always gregarious, a story teller. In the year leading up to my mother's death the stories at first grew shorter, then he would stumble over names or forget the plot. My mother had always, it seemed, but at least for a couple of decades, covered for him, filling in the blank spaces until their voices became a tag-team and sounded as if they'd rehearsed every tired anecdote, every worn-out rime I'd heard since I was a boy.

About six months into our bi-monthly routine Dr. Alford greeted us as usual, enquired how my father had been feeling, if he noticed any changes in his daily activities, then told a benign joke about a woman who kept misplacing her car keys; the punch line was they were always in her hand or in the ignition. I chuckled because that had become an everyday event. Dad didn't get it.

He always smiled, even if he didn't catch the humor. That visit his affect was completely neutral, his responses as animated as one hearing a Burger King menu recited by a bored teenager making five bucks an hour.

When my father was distracted by a door closing down the hall and he looked away, the doctor cut me a look that said, "How long has he been like this?" His eyes narrowed with concern. After my father left the office on the arm of a young assistant, the doctor pulled me back inside. "That was surprising today, concerning. Keep a close eye on him. He's still driving, isn't he?"

"Locally," I said.

"Maybe it's time you took the keys away, explain to him it's not safe for him to drive anymore. He could get lost, or worse."

"Lost? That's already happened at least once. He drove around for two hours, he thought he was in a town he'd never been in before."

"How'd he get home?"

"He just happened on the police station and had the presence of mind to pull in and ask for help."

"I'll bet your mother was worried sick."

"My mother was hopping mad. He left her at Shop Rite."

"Oh, boy."

"Yeah, but she calmed down when she asked him if he had been scared. He took a look at both of us and asked 'what are you talking about? I never got lost in my life. If I saw a road once I'd remember it fifty years later.' And that was true, I'd seen him do it, enter a small town in Vermont or New Hampshire, spot a secondary road, and know exactly where it would take him—once upon a time."

*

During those months, conversations became a game, better still, a test of where my father might actually believe he was in time and space. "I can't remember," I'd say, "what year did you graduate High School, Dad?"

"Nineteen forty-three," he'd say without inflection or hesitation.

"What rank were you in the Army?"

"Staff Sargent."

"What'd'ya do in the war?"

"I oversaw a warehouse, supervised Pilipino workers, a few American G.I.s. When the war was over, I was left behind to dispose of uniforms impregnated with chemicals against chemical warfare attacks on our guys. When our troops left, I drove to a high point above Manila Harbor," he said, his voice more animated than I heard it in a long, long time. "I watched the troop ships, my guys, sail out for home and I sat in my jeep and cried, not going home."

I'd heard the same words many times since my childhood. They always stopped me cold. I could not imagine my father crying. But here he was, 23 again, and a long way from small town America. Years later, in the cedar chest in the attic where his uniform and my mother's wedding dress lay locked in the past, I found a small book, issued by the U.S. Government to deployed troops in the event they were lost or captured. It was titled simply *Tagalog*, the language of the Philippines, a brief survival guide of words and phrases. In the back of the book, on blank pages, my father kept a kind of diary over a few awestruck days upon arrival. Notes. Impressions. But they were the only glimpses I had for years into the boy, young man, who would become my father after the war. Someone then who was capable of recording that he cried. An ability, or an honesty, hardened over by the time I was born.

When my maternal grandfather died in the early 80's, my father, my sister and I were the last to leave the room where my grandfather was laid out. It was the night before the funeral. The three of us stood at the door and said goodbye to the last visitors—old men and old women, and sometimes their children who came to pay respects in their stead.

"Good night. Good Night. Thank you for coming."

Now the room was empty except for the three of us. The funeral director lurked out of sight. We didn't speak. Stoic. We had done our job for the evening, for the past week. Bonnie had insisted that she would be a pall bearer. My father resisted, but my sister stood firm. "I'm as strong as any of you." He relented. We had talked to dozens of people we didn't know, heard stories we had or hadn't heard. We smiled, shook hands and were pleasant despite every impulse to shrink away and weep.

There are many sighs: Exasperation; Anger; Defeat; Disgust; Desolation. We together sighed a sigh of exhaustion. The poet Pablo Neruda wrote once, "I happen to be tired of being a man," or something like that. And that's how I felt, my first real funeral. My first real loss. And I'm sure my sister and father felt about the same.

For the first time in several days we stood alone in the semi-dark of the funeral home, ten actual yards but an unfathomable distance from a dead man we loved. The next day I would say a eulogy, my first. Writing it that afternoon I had stumbled over words and phrases and images I wanted to get right. In the hour before dressing for the funeral home, I flipped back through the pages of words, many x'd or crossed out. Over the hours of writing my penmanship had changed. The last few pages were a slow transformation of my clear, steady hand to something very like my grandfather's cramped, crabbed letters, small and somehow antique looking. I only shook my head.

We turned to leave. My father stopped, turned back toward the casket where my grandfather lay in his best suit. "Goodnight, Pop," he said, without design or decoration.

*

My mother's first heart attack was minor, but it set off sirens and bells to her doctors. Her fatigue and lack of stamina (she'd never had much) began to make sense to Bonnie and me. She had cooked almost every day my entire life. Now she made meals once, maybe twice, a week, the rest of the time it was lun-din at a few favorite restaurants and diners. She nibbled on fruit cups and salads, the occasional shrimp cocktail, but never a full meal—I hadn't seen her eat what most people would call a meal in years. Dad cruised along on clam strips and French fries, soup, well done steak and baked potatoes—God help us, hold the sour cream.

At seventy-five a doctor told my father he had the heart, stamina and body of a healthy fifty-year-old. But things were changing in his eighties, although he was still very strong. He still cut grass—for himself and a few "old people," –gardened and generally kept his yard in park-like order. It was not unusual for people driving through their small, old neighborhood to stop and ask to be shown around, though it was more likely he who offered the grand tour. He never turned anyone away. They may have been strangers or recent transplants passing through when they stopped, but when they left an hour or two later they were friends—schooled in his life, his town, his township, his history and that of his ancestors going back nearly four hundred years on the east coast. And they'd come back for more. After giving one lady the "three-hour tour," she invited him to her high school history class every year to speak as a living emissary from the past. At the end of a decade the class visit had become a yearly, day-long, school-wide gathering of

WWII vets who spent hour after hour, in classrooms and an auditorium, reminiscing about the war and the Greatest Generation. He was rarely happier.

So, my mother's home-cooked meals had become the exception rather than the rule. My father never complained, he just quietly packed on the restaurant pounds. Bonnie took over kitchen duties for a while, interrupting the late life romance with diner fare. But when she died, it was back to the routine—and the pounds.

At one point a month or two after Bonnie's death, I decided it would be a good idea to teach my father how to prepare three or four easy meals—meatloaf, stew, roasted chicken and macaroni and cheese. There was some variety and many fewer calories than the same dishes at the diner. Coupled with a salad and fresh or frozen vegetables from his garden they would both eat better, save money and calories and not run the nightly risk of disaster his (and her) erratic driving constantly threatened.

On the appointed Saturday I went shopping for the ingredients for all four meals with enough left over for one or two more lunches. I lugged four over-stuffed bags into the kitchen and leaned against the counter.

"Hi," Dad said from his seat at the kitchen table.

"Hi, Dad. Hi, Mom."

"What's in the bags," he asked.

"All the stuff for your cooking lesson."

He cut his eyes toward my mother in a panic. "It's all right, Warren, Jack is going to teach you how to make a few dishes."

"But I don't want to learn how to cook. I'm too old," he said as if I weren't there.

"We set this up weeks ago, so you could take some of the burden off of Mom."

He closed his eyes and shook his head. "Nobody told me about this."

"Should I just go home and leave all of the meat and vegetables to go bad?"

"Take them home with you, you bought them."

He had me for the moment. There was no reason I couldn't take it all home for Caitlin and me. Dad shook his head again and went back to his Word Find puzzle. Those and solitaire were now his chief forms of entertainment. He stopped watching television shows, at least those with plots, because he could no longer follow for more than a minute or two before he lost the thread or forgot who the characters were. His greatest power of concentration and recall came during those simple, solitary acts where everything around him seemed to disappear into a fog and it was just him and the cards or the book and pencil. One time when he set the deck of cards down while we waited for my mother to come out of surgery, I picked them up and laid out a game of solitaire. At first my father paid no attention, as I tended to ignore his games, but slowly he grew tired of watching the boats on the river and looked at what I was doing. Once or twice I glanced at him and his eyes were intent on my hands and movements. He didn't speak, he only watched, and I thought nothing of it. He often became almost mesmerized and stared at something invisible to the rest of us.

"What's that you're doing? he asked, genuinely curious.

"Just playing a hand of solitaire." I thought the question might be sarcastic. "Do you want the cards back?" the hand already lost.

"No," he said, "that looks very hard."

"What? You play hundreds of hands a day."

"How can that be? I don't know the rules. I don't think I ever played in my life."

"You just stopped playing five minutes ago."

"Jack, goddamnit, stop lying and trying to make me feel stupid." He tapped his fingers on his forehead when he said that, a new habit, and one, at some conscious or unconscious level, was designed to get him out of all manner of confusing situations, or at least to seek some sympathy.

"I'm not lying to you, Dad." I handed him the deck and he immediately laid out a hand and went back to playing. For a second, I thought it might have been a trick to get his cards back, but that flash of anger a moment ago had been for real. I sat back and watched him. The concentration was the look of a carefree, a truly carefree man giving himself over completely to the game. I sat for a long time, because time was all we had, and watched him deal hand after hand, no change in his look whether he won or lost. The game itself was all that mattered, one of his last anchors keeping him from drifting away, from disappearing forever from us.

"I'm not going straight home," I lied. The vegetables might keep for a few hours, but the meat will spoil." Like most people who lived through the Great Depression the very mention of waste, especially food, brought them to agitation that bordered on panic. His hand hovered over the book. His eyes twitched ever so slightly. My mother eyed us both, not taking sides.

"Well, you did promise to teach me how to make meat loaf. You're not trying to renig, are you? No hint of a smile. My mother slowly wagged her head. She would never get used to the breakneck changes in mood and memory Alzheimer's caused.

"Well then let's get after it, daddy-o," I said, unwilling to acknowledge his 180 degree turn around. I moved to the refrigerator and began pulling out packages of meat and laying them on the counter. He came and stood beside me, watching, as if I were pulling rabbits out of a hat. Except for salad I don't think I ever witnessed my father making a meal. Soup, maybe, out of a can, sandwiches, but nothing that required a sharp knife or mixing ingredients together in a bowl or pot or pan.

"What do I do?" he asked as innocently as a child.

"Start by washing your meat hooks, and so will I."

"But they're not dirty."

"You'd be surprised. Humor me, I'm the teacher." He gave his hands a cursory rinse and dried them on a paper towel. I was glad he hadn't chosen to use his pants legs.

"Okay," I said, "ready?"

"Ready. I'll watch." I thought about the game of solitaire but didn't bring it up. What for?

Right. We start by opening the packages of ground beef." I opened them with a knife and plopped all pound and a half of pink ground up cow in a mixing bowl. "Hand me one or two eggs, would you."

"Which will it be?"

"Two. Sorry. I'll try to be more precise." He nodded, stone faced. I cracked the eggs and dumped them on top of the meat. "Now, where do you keep the bread crumbs?" He shrugged. "Mom, where do you keep the bread crumbs?" I called into the living room.

"Cabinets on the left, top shelf."

"Next, we'll add the bread crumbs, salt and pepper, and my secret ingredient. Don't tell Mom," I whispered. He zipped his lips. "Good man," I said. Hint of a smile. "Now comes the fun part, want to play?"

"With that?" he asked pointing to the bowl.

"Yeah. That's why you washed your hands, so you could mix all that together."

"No," he said, his lip raised on one side in a look of disgust.

"How are you ever going to make meat loaf, or hamburgers, or meat balls if you won't mix the meat and eggs and all?"

He looked at me and shook his head very slowly. The look would have conveyed sympathy and understanding—had I been two years old again.

"You do it, I'll watch."

"But what will you do when I'm not here?"

"We'll go out like we always do."

But you're trying to get away from that, trying to save money. Restaurants, even diners, can get very expensive five or six times a week."

"Don't I know it," he said, "so show your mother how to do it. She *likes* doing this stuff." His eyebrows arched.

I plunged my hands into the meat and massaged the ingredients together. "You watching?"

"I am, and I'm glad those are your hands and not mine. Yech."

I dumped the mixture into a low casserole dish and shaped it into a loaf. I was happy to have the physical exertion to vent my anger. He wanted to learn to cook, he didn't want to learn to cook, he didn't want to keep going out to eat five nights a week, yet he didn't want to get his hands dirty—a man who worked his whole life with his hands. Who washed up at lunch time and the end of the day, and the rest of the time his hands were some degree of dirty.

*

With the meat loaf in the oven, topped with ketchup and three strips of bacon—"when the bacon is done, the meat loaf is done," I remembered hearing from my mother and my grandmother. Traditions. Ha!

"How's about we make some macaroni and cheese?" I asked him as cheerily as possible.

"Do you make it like your mother makes it? Any secret ingredients? I don't like that boxed stuff. Put in lots of Velveeta," he said. "Little boy cheese I call it." And he did, forever and always and every time we served it to him.

"Well, I don't use Velveeta. I use up whatever chunks of cheese are in the fridge, so it tastes different every time. But we don't waste any cheese. You'll like it," I said, knowing full well he wouldn't, and we would wind up making a second batch with Velveeta. Any swerve from the familiar was a non-starter. It was going to be Velveeta or mashed potatoes. A mélange of sharp, Swiss and bleu cheese were not going into any mac and cheese that was destined for his mouth.

"No, I won't. It's like you grew up in somebody else's house. What's wrong with how your mother makes it?"

"There's nothing wrong with it. I just thought you might like to try my recipe."

"Why?"

"Why what?"

"I know what I like, I like my mother's clam chowder, and her homemade bread. I like your mother's mac and cheese, her stew and . . . and some other things. You know. Make those, I'll watch."

"You're not going to learn? Mom can't do this anymore. She's sick, remember?"

"She is not. You're just saying that. Doris," he called into the living room, "your son says you're sick, set him straight, will ya?"

"I am sick, Warren. And I'm Grace. Doris was your mother."

"You don't feel good? Maybe we can make you some chicken soup or something. Do you want to go to bed? I'll help you up."

"It's cancer, Warren," exasperation tightening her throat, "bed and your damned chicken soup is not going to help." It was muffled, but I heard her crying. Sorry, Jack. I'm sorry."

"Hardly your fault, Mom."

Impatient, Dad looked at me. So, are we going to make the damned mac and cheese or what?"

"Yeah, yeah, we'll make it, with Velveeta, how would that be?"

"Great," he said, smiling, "your mother used to make it like that, I think. Little boy cheese she called it. Oh, that was years ago when you were just knee high to a grasshopper. That was dinner sometimes. Mac and cheese and some Big Boy tomatoes from the garden. Hot damn, that was a meal. Meat loaf was a luxury right after the war." He made that strange clicking, snapping sound that comes from pulling your tongue away from your gum at the side of your mouth. "Now we eat pancakes for supper. Can't remember the last time I had meat loaf."

I decided to take the chicken and stew beef home with me. Cooking class cancelled. Meat loaf and mac and cheese. "You want salad, Mom," I called out.

"Please," she said faintly. "Fruit."

I went into the living room and knelt by her chair. "Thanks for trying," she said. "I miss Bonnie so much. And he doesn't even remember."

He!

All week my father worked in a factory. When he came home to dinner at four p.m., the meal was ready for him, for us. Often times, in warmer months, after a quick meal he would leave again and paint houses until dark. As a boy, when he did not have a house to paint, we would sit on the front porch where my job was to pick solder, little silver BB's off his pant legs and T-shirt.

Sometimes on Sunday, if he did not have a second job, or a third job to go to, or a grave to dig, he and I would hike from our valley to the top of the hill where my grandparents lived. He would borrow an old cast iron frying pan from my grandmother, then we'd walk to the sand pit behind the cemetery. There we would build a fire pit and fry bacon. He hung the cooked strips on a nearby bush limb to drip. In the bacon grease he fried eggs and made toast.

We stuffed ourselves. He cleaned the cooled pan with a handful of sand. Then it was time to explore the woods, the old Lenape campground and Wilson pond—hand dug by my grandfather, my father and his brother during the Depression. We walked the pan back to my grandmother and hiked down the hill to home.

October 2009

Bonnie had been our parent's de facto caregiver for a couple of years. She lived next door in the only rental within blocks so that she could be there anytime within a few minutes and stay as long as she was needed. Now our parents were alone and it wasn't going well. Every doctor's appointment, every outing to the store, post office or restaurant was a nail biter until they called to announce themselves home safely and in for the night.

Bonnie's death was a trigger. Hers had been a steadying hand on the household even though both would have denied it. Was her presence important? God, yes. Could they get along without her cooking, cleaning, running to the store, to the doctor's? We'll show you, they seemed to say, closing ranks. We built this family. Raised you kids. We can keep going despite the sadness. They put on a brave face. And that lasted about a month. Then came the call early in the morning. My mother could not get out of bed. Caitlin and I lived two hours away. Dad was nagging her to get up, to make coffee and breakfast. But she physically couldn't get out of bed. He got angry. "Talk to him, please," she said over the phone, "try to explain."

She handed Dad the phone and for ten minutes I talked to my father as if he were a child. Logic and reason did not break through. Not only was he in an unfamiliar place, but unfamiliar things were happening—he was in a fog—at night. I tried to prod him into remembering stories from my boyhood to calm him down. I got him to remember Little League games half a century and more ago. Cub Scouts. Boy Scouts. Camping trips—he was a scout leader even before I was born. When I asked him if he remembered the woods fire (he became a volunteer fireman before I was born too) he calmed just a little, went back to that time for a few moments.

Then, "She won't get out of bed, Jack. I'm hungry."

"I know, Dad. Mom would get up if she could."

41

"I tried to help her, but she just lays there. I never learned how to cook an egg, or bacon. Maybe I did know, but I don't now. I'm getting stupid, Jack. (I imagined him tapping his forehead). Sometimes I wake up and there's fog all around me, even in the house. It scares me. Your mother sweeps it away. But now she won't get out of bed."

While I kept him busy on the phone, Caitlin called 911. "It's okay, Dad. Someone is coming to help you."

"Is Bonnie coming over. We haven't seen her in a few days."

"No, not Bonnie, Dad. Some people are coming to help Mom get out of bed, to get you some coffee and a hard roll."

"A Jersey breakfast. That'll be great."

"Yes, it will. They'll be there soon. Let them in when they ring the door bell, okay?"

"Oh, sure. I'll keep an eye out for them. Thanks, Jack. Coffee and a hard roll, hot damn." He clicked, tongue snapping from upper palette.

"Listen, I have to make some phone calls. I'm going to hang up. I'll call you back in a few minutes."

"Oh, sure. Call me back. Sure. Bye, Jack." I hung up reluctantly.

"They're on their way," Caitlin said.

"Now what?" I asked her. "Where will they go? They can't stay in the house. Bonnie was the only reason they could stay at home. Now what?"

Bonnie's death had rocked us to our heels. We knew their time alone without assistance and supervision was short, but we hadn't anticipated this. Side effects, yes, but not this sudden onset of whatever it was. There was no 800 number for magic answers. No shameless astrologer my mother spent exorbitantly on. She could not sit up, swing her legs over the side of the bed, walk to the kitchen. In the night something had shifted, some stars had fallen out of alignment, "someday" had walked into the house without knocking.

"Do you think it's physical?" I asked Caitlin. She put her hand on my arm.

"Maybe she's just had enough."

42

*

So that was it. After sixty-five years in their home they could no longer stay there safely on their own. And it was now up to me to find a safe place even though both of them had included in their living wills that they did not want to be placed in a nursing home. But what were the options?

"Senior apartments," Caitlin said as if reading my mind.

I went blank and just stared at her. I grew up in that township but couldn't recall ever seeing *senior* apartments. "Where would we find one of those?" She quickly rattled off the names of three different complexes with words like Towers and Arms in their names. I was familiar with them all but had never made a senior connection. "What makes them specifically for seniors?" I asked my new-found expert on all things senior.

"I'm only guessing here, but they probably have on-site nurses, CNA's," she stopped, probably because of the look on my face. "Certified Nursing Assistants."

"Oh, that would be good, huh?"

"Maybe there is a dining room, some special accommodations for wheel chairs and walkers. Like I said. I'm guessing, or maybe just hoping."

Without waiting for me to ask, Caitlin picked up the phone and dialed her brother who still lived near my parents. When he picked up, she went straight to the problem. "Hi, Ken. We have a situation with Jack's parents. What do you know about . . . and she ticked off the names of the three complexes to him. "Any of them fallen into disrepair? Any have a better reputation than the others? Uh huh. Thanks, can you look up those phone numbers for me? I'll call you back in ten. Bye."

"Okay," she said, "Ken's looking up the numbers. Call your father and tell him not to worry, we're working on some things, they'll be all right. Tell him we'll meet him at the hospital. Find out if the ambulance has arrived."

I was on auto pilot and I did as I was told. But my mind was still racing. Even if we found a safe apartment, we would still have to move their life from a 2000 square foot house to a 700 square foot apartment. And what about their attic, the basement, shed, garage—all bulging with a lifetime of accumulation? With the new semester only weeks away, how were we going to accomplish everything it would normally take months or a year?

Caitlin took over. She didn't ask if I needed help, she knew that I needed help. She called her brother back, wrote down the telephone numbers, hung up and immediately called the first senior complex on the list and spoke with a representative. "Yes," she reported to me, "they have a one bedroom available—in two weeks after paint, repairs, that sort of thing."

"What would we do in the meantime?"

"Good question."

"Let me call the other two places," Caitlin said, "then we need to get to the hospital."

"You know," I said, "we could look at places closer to us. We're not restricted to their township or county even. Who are we trying to be considerate of? We're it. End of the line."

"True enough," she said, shushing me with her palm as someone answered her second call.

I had explained the situation to the 911 operator, so I was sure the EMT's had taken him with my mother in the ambulance. We couldn't expect the ER staff to keep an eye on him, but I was reasonably certain he would not leave Mom's side once they were in the hospital.

Alzheimer's patients frequently wander, hence the double and triple security measures inside of designated Alzheimer's units. Wandering grows out of boredom and disorientation, a desire to get home. But the stimulation and unfamiliar confusion of a hospital was probably enough to keep Dad glued to my mother's side. That, and not a little bit of fear, a very new experience for my father.

"The second place, Brisbane Towers, has a one-bedroom unit, second floor, with elevator, that has just been refurbished. Move in tomorrow. They have nurses on staff, a dining room, activities, a movie night, music, you name it. Hell, I'd like to live there."

"And the last place on the list?"

"Same as the first. Two weeks at least until move-in is possible."

"Okay, let's wait and see what the doctors have to say. They might say they need to go straight to a nursing home. Jesus, this is the stuff of nightmares."

"Yup."

"Then not too far down the road we're going to have to think about emptying the house out, putting it on the market. Doesn't Medicare or Social Security require you to liquidate everything?"

"I don't know the specifics, but that sounds about right. Makes sense anyway. There's probably a web site for that. We can get Jon to check it out for us."

We said little the rest of the way to the hospital, both of us overwhelmed by the storm blocking ahead of us and with no way to the other side but through it.

*

We found Dad sitting beside my mother's bed. She was sitting up, he was holding her hand and looking out the window. Mom smiled when we came around the curtain, Dad looked up like we had just stepped out of the room and were returning.

"Hey," I said, "you've got to stop cooking up ways to get us down from our mountain to your beach." Mom smiled again.

"Believe me, I'm running out of ways to be creative."

"Oh, sure," I said and winked.

"Grace couldn't get out of bed to fix my breakfast today. And I was hungry. So, I know she wasn't trying to play a trick on you."

"I know, Dad, I was joking with her." For a while I found it odd that he had stopped calling my mother Mom when talking to Caitlin or me, and sometimes even Jon.

"Okay," he said. While he was talking, he had stopped rubbing the back of my mother's hand like a worry stone. He started again, the old story teller's words exhausted. Caitlin stood behind him and rubbed his shoulders, once straight, now collapsed like an ancient bridge. Just a

45

few years ago, when we stood side by side, it was hard to see the difference between his six-foot height and my six foot two. Now his head barely rose above my shoulder. The half inch in height per decade he should have lost, but didn't, had come all in a rush, and in just two years he had settled into his new self, a quiet, private and perhaps unwitting surrender to the many forces he must have felt, if only in rare, lucid moments, had gathered against him. If we, who could clearly organize and analyze the seemingly endless assaults against our family, felt bushwhacked and dizzy, I could only imagine how my father felt deep in the isolation of his disease. Deaths, though quickly forgotten, and illness he was confronted with daily were more insults added to the morning shock of waking into an almost unknown world, peopled with those he knew he knew but could not name.

"Jon's here," my mother said, "somewhere. I think he went for coffee or tea. He offered to bring your father some."

"How long were you here before Jon got here?" Caitlin asked.

"He was waiting for us. He beat the ambulance by about ten minutes, he told us." She beamed. Jon was her first grandchild, the only grandchild as it turned out. She kept his picture on her night stand, changed it every year until it must have seemed like one of those books you hold by the spine and rifle the pages and the images leap from stillness to motion. In her magic book of memories my son grew from an infant to a man in only seconds. And I understand that magic, it tricks me too—every day.

"So, what did the doctor's find?" I asked.

"They ran more tests, of course. Took my blood." She held up her arm, bruised from wrist to armpit. "They took a bunch of x-rays of something." She hung her head. "Sorry I had to call you this morning. I tried to explain what was happening to your father, but he just kept saying he wanted his breakfast. I know he doesn't understand what's going on, but I got angry, it can't always be about him. I told him to go sit in his chair and watch the news, play solitaire. I told him…to leave me alone."

"I want you to call us anytime. If we're not home, call Jon."

"I know, but…"

"But nothing. We love you. This is what we do. You did for Bonnie and me all those years. Now it's my turn."

"Okay."

"And it's okay to feel angry, maybe even a little betrayed. But it's the disease, not the man who's betrayed you. But you know all that."

"I do, but it's good to hear it reinforced sometimes, to hear some common sense."

"I know. They didn't tell us when we bought into this contraption that a boat load of assembly was required." I said.

She narrowed her eyes. "What contraption? I don't follow."

"Life," I told her, "it was a clumsy figure, sorry."

Just then Jon walked in with a cardboard tray of cups—coffee, and most of it decaf owing to the time of day, but still high octane for his grandfather. Jon once admiringly said to me he had never known anyone else who could fall asleep drinking a cup of caffeinated coffee. "How does he do that?" he wanted to know.

I for one was thankful for the distraction, a chance to sip and watch sailboats fly over the chop on the river. "Helluva view," I said to my mother.

"Million dollar," she said without smiling. We all knew she'd rather be in her landlocked home, miles from river and ocean.

Mom and Dad both drifted off to sleep at mid-afternoon. So, Caitlin, Jon and I stepped out.

"Early dinner?" I suggested.

"I'm not very hungry," Caitlin said, "But I could go for a glass of Merlot. Jon?"

"I wouldn't say no to a beer and a burger."

"Good. Any suggestions? There are mostly only new places around anymore. So yuppified. Any of the old joints still around?" I asked.

"Don't know," Jon said. "It's all changed since I used to hang out in this town."

"Ditto," said Caitlin with a smile.

47

"Whataya say we just walk up town and see what's what?" I said.

"Fresh air and a leg stretching. Sounds good to me. Let's go."

We walked up Broad Street stopping at some of the new cafes and bistros with their menus in glass boxes outside the entrances. "Jesus, I just want a burger and some suds, I don't need an 'experience'," Jon said.

"I'm with you, my boy." Caitlin ran her finger down the glass. "I don't even know what half this stuff is, and I'm the sophisticated one in the bunch."

"I heard if you can't pronounce it, they can charge more for it. If it's crap, it's your fault for ordering it," Jon told his mother.

"And most people won't complain; it's not a cool thing to do," I added. "I'll stick with a burger or a slice."

"A slice," Jon echoed me, "that sounds better than a burger. So right this way, I know just the spot."

It was quaint, that is to say, small and dark with some dusty old wine bottles on the window sills for ambience. Very soft music escaped from the kitchen, accompanied by two voices. We were the only customers. I supposed they didn't often entertain anyone at two in the afternoon on a weekday, so the server was surprised when she pushed through the old fashion barroom doors into the dining area.

"Oh. Have you been here long?"

"Only a couple of minutes, not to worry" I said to her.

"This is usually a dead time. Time to get ready for the dinner rush," she said, smiling. "Not. We haven't had a rush in a while."

"We saw a lot of bistros and trattorias on Broad Street."

She rolled her eyes. "Yeah, not the same town I grew up in. What'll it be?"

"Two beers and a Merlot," I told her.

"Chianti be all right?" Caitlin nodded

"Be right back. Water?"

✳

48

"You just missed the doctor," Mom greeted us when we returned from lunch. Dad nodded.

"So, what did he say?" Dad shrugged. Mom had a puzzled look on her face.

"She. And not too much. She said they ran blood tests, which I already knew," she said holding up her bruised arm again. X-rays showed no reason why my legs refused to work this morning." She went silent.

"What else?" Jon asked.

"Well," she glanced at my father, "she said it was a mystery."

"A mystery?" Jon shot back.

"A mystery, that's exactly what she said," Mom said to Jon defensively.

"Once again, modern medicine to the rescue. Does anyone else feel lucky to be alive right now in this age of scientific wonder cures? Bullshit, sorry Grandma, but this is pure bullshit."

"You're right, Jon. Makes you wonder if the 'cure rates' quoted on those TV commercials is based on isolated cases. A mystery, really?"

"That's what the lady told me. I'm not making this up."

"Didn't think you were, Mom. We're just all very frustrated and . . ." I stopped. Looked at Caitlin, took a deep breath and changed my tack. "Are they going to get you up and on your feet?"

"Tomorrow. I have a physical therapy session at ten."

"Good." I turned around and saw my father shrinking away from all the talk he didn't understand. He had moved from bedside to a chair, then slid the chair into a corner. *You can run*, I thought. "Come on, Dad, join us. Mom's going to be okay." I tried to lighten up, but I didn't fool anyone. I know, I hadn't even fooled myself. I felt like I'd been sucker punched in the gut.

"Did you get the doctor's name?" Jon asked his grandmother.

"No," she said sheepishly, "she talked too fast. She was in and out in just a few minutes. The nurse stayed when the doctor left, but she was busy too with all these machines and I didn't want to bother her."

"Her job is to be bothered," Jon said. My father cut him a wilting look. "Sorry, Grandpa, I'm upset."

Caitlin got up at some point during the exchange and left the room. Only Dad seemed to have noticed.

"Where's Mom?" Jon finally asked. Dad threw a hitch hiker thumb down the hall towards the nurse's station which he could see from his corner. I went to the door, mid-way down the hall Caitlin stood talking calmly to a woman in a long white doctor's coat. *We'll know something soon enough.*

Mom was, at this point, in her fifth or sixth year of chemo therapy. Weak would not begin to describe her physical state. She was frail. Her cheeks were sunken, and her hair had fallen out so many times, then grown back strange colors and textures, she looked like someone I did not know, far from the robust woman who raised me. Had I met her in a store or restaurant having not seen her in six months, I might not have recognized her. My own mother.

Dad had given me a hard time when I was younger and grew my hair long. Now he had a mane of white hair. He used to take himself to the barber religiously every month. Now it was two, three, even four months between haircuts, combed straight back, it cascaded to his collar and over his ears—we called him "the Lion in Winter." He looked the same as he always had in his later years, only shorter, older and paler. When he forgot to put his teeth in, his face collapsed from nose to chin.

Like many Alzheimer's patients he was beginning to shy away from basic hygiene. Mom would help him undress down to underwear, drape a fresh towel over his arm, turn on the shower and send him in to bathe on his own. He would close the door, sit on the toilet, lid down, and wait until he had faked a shower long enough. Water off, he returned to the bedroom thinking, somehow, my mother would be fooled.

He'd announce, "All done." Mom would touch his skin, feel the towel, look at his hair, not even a little damp.

"Why don't you want to shower any more, Warren?"

"I did shower, you saw me come out of the bathroom."

"I did, and I heard the shower running. But no one was under the water. Your skin is dry. The towel is dry. Your hair is dry, and too long." And then he'd get mad.

"Are you saying I'm lying to you, Grace?"

"I'm saying you're not telling me the truth."

"That's lying. I took a shower, now let me get my clothes on."

"You shouldn't put clean clothes on a dirty body."

"Now I'm dirty?"

"You're not clean. You didn't shower."

And so it went, sometimes days at a time. I was happy never to be privy to one of those confrontations, discussions, or whatever they were. They tested my mother unlike anything I'd seen before. She had always been patient with her children, and with my father's obsessive (in his younger days) civic engagements, whether with scouts, politics, or the fire company, and later with his speaking dates with high school students about his experiences in the War. These tried her patience but did not win. But this, this resistance to showering, even washing his hands, was too much. It was never stated, or at least I never heard it stated, but I believe that this aversion, call it a tick, maybe, was the final trial that precipitated their taking separate bedrooms. True, Dad was a heavy sleeper, and Mom was an insomniac, or at best, a very light sleeper, but they had worked around those differences for sixty plus years. So, it surprised us all to find they now occupied bedrooms across the hall from each other. Dad seemed happy to have space for his coins and coin books. Mom was thrilled the have closet space freed up for all the clothes she bought, but more often than not, never wore.

Changes were wrought so slowly in their home that it was hard to spot how things had become somehow different from what they'd always been. Hadn't Dad always worn long sleeve shirts? (No). Hadn't Mom always tucked a Kleenex into the cuff of her cardigan sleeve? (No, but her mother had.) Hadn't there always been overflow groceries stacked around the kitchen island? Hadn't there always been collections of glassware, pewter and brass displayed on every available horizontal surface from the kitchen to the living room? (No, and no.)

Growing up in that house in the fifties and sixties, Bonnie and I had experienced that era's stripped down, shiny, clean-lined modernism, that is until the "colonial" furnishings, wall paper, and eagles, eagles everywhere took over what seemed like every house in mid-sixties America. Looking back, it seems clear that this was the genesis of the return to fears engendered by the Great Depression. Houses, most not as quickly and thoroughly as ours, began to fill up with stuff. Collections of dizzying variety. As a boy I was encouraged to collect match-book covers—I had several albums full. Bonnie collected salts, tiny little bowls that predated salt shakers for dispensing, what else, salt—and she had hundreds. My parents began collecting art glass and pewter, and in a few short years they expanded their buying to anything that caught their fancy. (This was, made flesh, their "retirement fund," albeit one they could enjoy looking at and handling until such time it became necessary to liquidate.) If Big Band 78's ever came back into fashion, they'd have had a corner on the market. Boxes of them hunkered in the attic like potatoes in a root cellar.

In college I first read in Ovid's *Metamorphosis* a depiction of the "Golden Age" as the "damned desire of having." *Ovid must have known my parents*. So, the house went from lean and clean to more over stuffed than a Victorian sofa.

The change had been slow, a decade, but thorough. And it was only when I returned home from grad school that the transformation became obvious. My parents were officially collectors of the first order—if not hoarders of the third or fourth order.

The doctor, as it turned out, Dr. Lois Goodyear, had not told my mother that her condition was a mystery. She told Caitlin that she had, in fact, said that these kinds of temporary paralyses appeared mysteriously sometimes—and disappeared just as quickly and mysteriously. Mysterious, yes, but hardly unheard of. Caitlin told me the doctor apologized for the misunderstanding. And yes, the visit had been brief because they were one doctor short on the shift. Caitlin thanked her, and Dr. Goodyear promised to return to Mom's room and try to explain what was happening just as soon as she could.

Jon visibly calmed and apologized to both of his grandparents. Mom forgave him and kissed his cheek. Dad nodded, his flash of anger long forgotten. I pulled a chair up next to my father and inaugurated one of my reality check conversations. "So, Dad, what sport did you most enjoy playing in high school?"

"Oh, basketball, I suppose. Though I was also a cross country runner."

"You weren't very tall for a basketball player, huh?"

"I sure was. Six foot. Only two guys taller than me. By an inch. Bob Cousy, 'Houdini of the hardwood' they used to call him, was six foot too, and a pro. Boston Celtics."

"And what years did you play?" "Nineteen forty-one and forty-two. Then I graduated, got drafted into the Army after Pearl Harbor."

"You remember a lot."

"I remember everything worth remembering," he said, tapping his forehead.

"Then you've got a head full of good memories. I've heard a lot of them. You had a good life."

"Oh, yes. Still do. Good memories. Locked up here." He tapped his forehead again. "Safe as a safe." But I let it pass.

"So, Mom's going to be all right," I told him. He nodded, flashed half a smile. Click.

Caitlin explained to my mother the conversation she'd had with Dr. Goodyear. Told her she probably mis-heard "Mysterious" and thought "mystery." At any rate, no harm done worse than an hour of unnecessary worry, and an upset grandson. The doctor would be back to see her later.

"So, I'm not a mystery," my mother mused, "darn, what a shame." She cut her eyes toward Caitlin. "Always wanted to be." Caitlin laughed and winked at her.

My father, sensing that something had changed in the room while he and I talked basketball and WWII, pulled his chair back closer to the bed.

*

By the next morning my mother's legs were working as they always had. "Well, that was weird," she remarked when she returned from physical therapy. "I hope that never happens when I'm crossing a street," she joked.

"Should I expect that to happen again?" she told us she had asked the therapist. He told her that was a question for the doctor; he was there to get her back on her feet, and hopefully keep her there.

She looked very relieved, even her face looked less drawn and gaunt. Although she had merely nibbled on lunch and dinner the day before, today she tucked into some tepid soup and half a tuna fish sandwich.

"I didn't know you could eat like that, Grandma," Jon said to her, amused.

"Neither did I, Jon. To be honest, I haven't been able to taste much for a couple of years, at least, but today, I don't know, I could taste and smell. Funny, it even felt good in my mouth. Do you think that's crazy?"

"Not at all. I think it's wonderful. Let's hope your senses stick around for a long time." He kissed his grandmother on the forehead. "Now, don't let me interrupt you."

Later, in the afternoon, we got down to business, to the conversation we needed, but dreaded, having. We hemmed and hawed and put it off, went for coffee, pretended whatever drivel was on the television required our absolute attention. Caitlin and I kept looking furtively at one another. Finally, my mother had had enough. "What's going on?"

"Well," I said, "we need to talk to you about a few things."

"Like?"

"Like going back home, to the house, just the two of you."

"And why wouldn't we, Jack?"

"Because what happened yesterday might happen again, or worse."

"Or worse? Like what?"

"What if your legs gave out and you fell? This time you lucked out and the temporary paralysis happened in your sleep, and all the pieces after that fell into place in the best possible way, and now you're here and safe."

"That's right," she said defensively.

"But next time…"

"If there is a next time. The doctor couldn't or wouldn't say."

"But what if you were at the top of the stairs? What if you were standing next to the stove with burners on? What if you were getting out of the car?"

"What if, what if, what if, Jack. I know you can be a worrier sometimes, but goodness sakes, don't you have a lecture to write, or papers to grade? I didn't worry that much when you cracked your head open playing pick-up football."

"Look, one way or another we all knew this was coming, sometime, somehow. We don't want this any more than you do. I grew up in that house. Every early, no no, every important memory of my first twenty-two years is somehow attached to that house one way or another." My mother began to cry. I watched her deflate, the fight not leaking but rushing out of her.

"We both have it in our living wills that we don't want to go to a nursing home," she said between sobs.

"You don't have to," I said, failing to add the obvious, "yet."

My father looked alarmed at seeing tears, and he looked to me, asking with his eyes and that slight tilt of his head, "what did you say?" his protective instinct intact, even if comprehension was not. In that instant my father confirmed what I had known all my life, he would die fighting—anyone! son or stranger—to protect his Grace. His expression, confused but clearly angry—and he was slow to anger— said 'Don't test me.' I had no intention.

The tears slowed over the next few minutes. Stopped. "What did you mean when you said we didn't have to go into a nursing home?"

"Caitlin?" I said.

"We've been looking into alternatives, something not so drastic as a nursing home. We don't think you need that—right now, and Dr.

Goodyear agrees, as long as there is help very nearby, you should be able to stay by yourselves."

My mother brightened just a little, as if her tears had somehow precipitated a small victory. A moment later her look suggested that maybe an unexpected adventure was in the offing, not exactly a cruise to the Caribbean or Alaska, but at least new walls to look at, new people to talk to.

"Where would this be?" she asked Caitlin, ignoring me for a moment of punishment.

"Only a few miles from your home," she told her, "in an apartment."

"Oh. We haven't lived in one of those since we were first married. I lived there alone while Warren was overseas."

"It'll be like a trip back in time," I put in, "but you won't have to cook because there is a dining room. There will be nurses on premises if you need them."

"How big is this apartment?"

"We went to see them. They're about 700 square feet. Just painted. New carpet. Nice."

"How big is our house?"

"About 1800 square feet, give or take."

"Jack, will we ever be able to move back home?"

"I don't know, Mom. We'll have to see what happens."

Wrong answer.

January 29, 2014

Who wouldn't want their father back? I woke from a dream of an old house, the roof caving in. The house stood in a woods—generic, no place I recognized—and a stream flowed nearby. These were all of the elements of a typical dream I'd been having for at least the past half dozen years. The plan, as best that I could reconstruct, was to rebuild the crumbling house, to…And that's where my insight and analysis broke down. *Crumbling house*. Please, I get it. *I like my dream-speak a little less obvious. Okay, toss in the stream, smart ass Id. How do you like that?*

Welcome back, Dad. How does the world look to you? Fresh and shiny after the long trek through the fog? Finally, a day dawning clear and familiar, no jumble of voices, strange streets, odd smells. Welcome to the familiar. Welcome home. We'll throw you a parade, how's that? A Birthday party, a born-again Birthday party. Christmas, St. Patrick's Day, 4th of July—all as you remember them. But by the way, a few people will be missing—your daughter, your wife. Oh, yes, and your home of six decades is gone. Sorry.

Caitlin snores softly beside me. For once I'm grateful for the distraction. For once I don't feel the need to get up, go to the living room, read. I want this intimacy without waking her up. Without touching.

The dream hangs between us. For years she has spoken in tongues in her sleep. Out of nowhere in the middle of the night she has babbled nonsense built on an intricate syntax for no apparent reason. The first time I heard it it woke me from a sound sleep. She commenced to jabbering, not one clear word of English or French or Spanish. Just gibberish. It shook me. I lay awake for hours afterword expecting there would be more. She simply snored.

Welcome back, Dad.

September 2009

Wrong answer indeed. Whatever hint of excitement had shown on Mom's face disappeared before the sound of my words went silent in the room— "we'll have to see what happens."

"What did you say to your mother to make her cry?"

"I told her the truth."

"About what?"

"About whether you'd ever be able to live in your house again."

"What are you talking about, damnit. There is not a thing wrong with that house. We've lived there for over twenty years."

"Sixty, Dad, no, sixty-five."

"Twenty years, sixty years. Who the hell cares? How long has this been going on behind my back, Grace?"

"Oh, Warren, nothing is going on behind your back. Jack and Caitlin and Jon think it's not safe for us to stay in the house alone for a while."

"Over my dead body, Jack. You're not taking my house away from me."

"No, we're not. And that dead body is what we're trying to prevent."

"I've been taking care of myself for eighty-eight years, and your mother for sixty-five, so you say, and I'll keep taking care of her as long as I draw a breath of life. You can't do this to us." Red faced, he staggered up out of the chair like he was going to swing at me, but he stopped short.

My mother stopped crying and dried her cheeks. "Hon. Warren, they aren't doing any of this to us, they're doing something for us. They don't want us to get hurt." She looked at me.

"That's right."

"Oh, for crying out loud." My father said. I don't know what's going on around here, but I sure plan to find out. He sat back down in the chair and inched it slowly back toward the corner, his face telling us he was already trying to remember what had just happened. It shook me to my core.

My mother stayed in the hospital three more days. The paralysis did not reoccur. We took Dad back to his house every evening. We stayed in what had been the nursery when I was born, and then again for Bonnie. It was now a guest room/catchall for the guests who never came and the possessions that overflowed the attic, basement, garage and any other places not designated for living. We moved and stacked boxes, bags, and loose garments to make room enough for us to sleep on an old double bed. At least that was the plan. We tried, but eventually we each grabbed a blanket and moved down to the living room to crash on recliners.

Each morning we drove my father back to the hospital after experiencing first hand his refusal to shower, or even wash much more than hands and face. He did soak his dentures overnight and comb his hair in the morning. Except for the showering he continued to follow the rituals of a lifetime. After dressing in slacks and a short sleeve shirt, he would systematically load his pockets: pen in his shirt pocket; coins in his right front pants pocket; a fresh white handkerchief in the left front—laundered and pressed by the dozens by my mother, so there was no fear of running out any time soon). Although I continued his practice of carrying a pocket comb in my right rear pants pocket into my teen years, I abandoned early his handkerchief habit (snot in my pocket never much appealed to me.) Finally, his wallet, molded over decades to the shape of his left glute, went into his left rear pocket. Ensemble complete, almost. He always wore a wristwatch on his left arm, and his wedding ring, a gold band worn thin as his war stories. On his head went the WWII Veteran's baseball cap adorned with replicas of his various medals and ribbons.

"Looking spiffy this morning, Sarge," I said to him. He grinned and snapped me a salute. "What'll it be today, coffee and a hard roll, or a hard roll and coffee?"

"A bunch of each, no matter how you want to serve them."

After dropping him off at the hospital and saying good morning to my mother, we dove into our new chore of choosing furniture for the apartment, renting a U Haul for the day, and delivering and (temporarily arranging) load after load to their new home. Funny, but Dad never seemed to notice, when we took him home in the evening, what pieces were missing, the tables, chairs, pictures, an entire bedroom set went without comment or concern.

On the final day before my mother was to be released from the hospital, we hired a couple of young, strong men to help with the sofa and recliners. (Where would we sleep? We didn't think of that.") They did the heavy lifting at the house and again at the apartment. We tipped them well.

That night Caitlin and I collapsed into whatever upholstered furniture remained and had no trouble sleeping the sleep of children dislocating their parents—fitful beyond exhaustion. Dad slept like the proverbial baby.

Tomorrow night, we promised each other, back at home it would be better. Jon laughed out loud when he heard us say that.

I have heard people try to rank the best and worst days of their lives. We, as a family had accumulated so many bad days in the past few years that we longed for days that fell, not at the opposite extreme, but in the vast middle ground of days never to be remembered. Moving day, as we had come to call it, was promising to be anything but normal and forgettable. For one thing, my mother had made us promise to take her home for a visit (not with neighbors, but with stuff) before proceeding to the apartment so she could "pick up a few things" we, no doubt, had forgotten. So be it. We would swing by 16 Mount Avenue for maybe half an hour, then move on to Brisbane Towers, Apartment 2 B, where we had worked very hard to make the surroundings familiar, unthreatening, yet not so familiar as to make them nostalgic and sad.

We left the hospital without incident or fanfare and drove more slowly than was usual—or safe—so my mother could "drink in" the trees and houses, the smells and sounds of the world not-hospital. So far, so good. We were in no hurry, Caitlin and I, to begin a homecoming that was to be brief, and, in fact, an anti-homecoming.

When we pulled into the driveway, my mother teared up. We had expected that, and why shouldn't she, I thought, this was quite possibly a farewell to a life she had embraced since Truman was in office, before children, hell, almost from before "the bomb" forced the entire world to live under the mushroom cloud. This had always been her safe place to retreat to after surgery or chemo, after my father's diagnosis, after the death of her daughter. This place was the treasure chest she and my father had filled up together. Hell yeah, she had a right to cry. And so did I if I chose to.

We went in through the side (basement) door, protected by a pergola my father had built ten, fifteen years ago before disease stole his skills. Up three stairs and we were in the kitchen with its picture window looking out over the side yard where I had played baseball as a kid. Although we had broken windows in the neighbor's house many times, the picture window was the same one, intact. There was the crowded island jammed with cereal boxes and twelve packs of soda and juice. On the kitchen table lay two Word-Find books and my father's well-worn pack of playing cards. On my mother's end was a neat pile of scrupulous to-do lists left to be completed the day her temporary paralysis knocked all good intentions asunder.

My mother did not, to our relief, weep. She was very calm and smiled as she moved through her rooms. Over the years I have come to divide our perceptions of the world into three unequal parts. We *see*: we all see every day. It is our most basic apprehension of the world, what keeps us from walking into walls or off of cliffs. We *witness*: we see, but with an added dimension. What we take in with our eyes has meaning beyond what keeps us safe and content all of our waking hours. Most people do this rarely. This is the condition of poets. We *behold*: this extraordinarily rare state approaches the ecstatic, a place most people get to visit once in their lives if they are very lucky. Most people go there never. Here the world and life itself makes sense in a flash of extremity, then vanishes leaving only a tingling trace of what occurred in a moment shorter than an eye blink. It is where saints and mystics and bodhisattvas dwell. But that was the look on my mother's face. On the brink of leaving home, she was truly seeing it, no, beholding it for what it was and what it meant to her and my father. I could only hold my breath and be thankful.

She moved like a child among her things, picking up and setting down pitchers, celery jars, plates, toothpick holders, cups, salts, fairy lamps, saucers and dozens of other glass items arrayed on hutch and chair rail, dry sink and shelves built into a defunct doorway. Pick up. Caress. Replace. Over and over.

I could only watch for so long. I turned to watch my father deal his cards into a hand of solitaire. He instantly tuned out everything else. He was back in the game. My mother moved wordlessly among the many things she had collected since my childhood. Some I remembered her buying, and where. Some had appeared—abracadabra—some were enchanted into their always place on shelf, table, once empty space.

The spell broke in a few minutes and my mother collapsed into her chair, exhausted, and not a little agitated. Our half hour visit to the home place had already stretched to an hour, and Mom melted into her space. Caitlin looked at me, what happened? I shrugged, the visit gently snatched out of my control. Damnit.

"Okay," I announced. "We have a meeting with Elizabeth at 2 p.m. We need to go."

"Who's Elizabeth?" my mother asked, suddenly suspicious.

"She's the director, the overseer, the land lady at your new apartment building," I told her, flustered.

"I need to gather a few things."

"Sure, Mom."

"My mother tatted this, embroidered this table cloth," she muttered. "I can't leave this. I couldn't sleep knowing this was left behind." She seemed determined to take everything.

The spell was broken. The beheld, the witnessed, was crammed into a few Johnny Walker and Popov boxes for the trip to "this-is-home-til-I-recover." She gathered anything and everything that she could blindly fit into a bundle of tissue paper and carry away.

Predictably, the ride to the Bainebridge Towers was quiet to the point of discomfort. I could hear my mother sobbing again in the back seat. I knew without turning around that my father was worrying the back of her hand with his thumb. Dad may have been stumbling through the daily fog of confusion, troubled to be riding on unfamiliar roads he had ironically known for nine decades, but he still knew when he was needed to console.

Like parents driving a daughter on a date, Caitlin and I refused to look in the back seat. A huge portion of the privacy they had enjoyed for so long, almost an anonymity, was about to be yanked from them. Strangers would know their losses and ailments. They would come and go from their apartment, from their building, under the eye of people whose names they did not know and who did not know them. I knew we were doing what we had to do, for a while at least, but the urge was to turn around and take them home to 16 Mount Avenue, to deposit them among familiar sights and familiar things. My mind raced trying to find some way, somehow, to make them happy—and safe on their own.

"This is how it has to be," Caitlin said softly as she watched my eyes dance as if in REM sleep.

The "meeting" with Elizabeth amounted to a greeting of my parents, a showing of the apartment, and a grand tour of the property with a stop for coffee and tea in the dining room and a general introduction to the community, offerings, expectations and the general sense of esprit de corp. My mother was discrete, but skeptical—not a joiner or a community participant. Dad might have relished all of this fifteen or twenty years ago, joining shuffleboard and canasta tournaments. But now, he seemed bored and distracted, happy only when they stopped for coffee. At times like these I wanted to cry and hug him like I was a five-year-old boy.

The tour complete, we retreated to the apartment. My mother smiled to see familiar things, though in massively diminished numbers. She immediately set about rearranging the small objects, pulled others from her shopping bag of tissue-wrapped things, and generally began to duplicate the clutter of home.

"Okay," I said, "does this seem like someplace you can call home?"

"This will never be home. This is a stopover." If looks could kill.

"Touché," I said. "A good way to look at it. A good place to recuperate and recover. How's that?" I said.

"Then we reevaluate."

I sucked in a huge breath. "Yeah, if that's how you want to think about it. Okay."

"I'm going home, Jack," she said fiercely. We let it go, Caitlin and I. Mom's speech of a few days ago about doing *for* them hung hollow as a campaign promise.

Jon had made their bed, placed bright night-lights in the bedroom, hall and bathroom. I made them tea and laid the TV remote on Mom's night table. They were tired but running on reserves that were decades deep. Even if Dad would drift off as soon as his head hit the pillow—any pillow, familiar or strange—Mom would fight it to the point of insomnia. Even if she slept, she'd swear she hadn't, swear she'd been awake since her first night in the hospital.

I'd watched her sleep, for hours. There was a type of insomnia I'd read about where the person would absolutely believe that they had not slept when they had. Not well, but for a while. She said no, she hadn't slept at all, she was just resting her eyes. I couldn't argue anymore. *Okay, you've been awake for 96 hours. You win.*

We left them that first night to figure it out. To establish a new routine. To sleep, to not sleep. The place was lit softly, even if the geography was still unfamiliar. It was not as if they drank and got confused. We had gone over the paths from bedroom to bathroom, bathroom to bedroom.

We left them that first night expecting the worst. Driving home, we expected to be driving back within hours to 2B, the new unwanted home.

*

Caitlin's cell phone had three wake-up alarm settings. The morning after The Move, she set them all. Each setting allowed for a five, ten- or thirty-minute pause between alarms. We dubbed them "the bells of good intentions," and a half hour later, "the bells of revised expectations," and thirty minutes (an hour) later, "the bells of earthy realities." We rode the alarm through all three alerts, finally giving up on any hope of oblivion when Jon called and wanted to know when we were heading to the apartment.

"Once we rise from the dead," I told him.

"Exit the tomb," he told me, "this is just the beginning."

When I was a boy, my grandmother had, in her basement, a machine called a mangler that squeezed moisture out of sheets and other clothes, then pulled them through, ironing them flat. That is how Caitlin and I felt following the paralysis, mangled, hospitalization and move to the apartment all in less than a week. We were mangled, done and undone all at once.

By the time we arrived on Thursday morning, day two in 2B, my mother had already compiled a shopping list of reasons why this was not her home and never could be. "Your father has no place to play with his coins," she greeted us when she answered the door.

"Sleep well?" I asked.

"Huh, not at all."

"Still riding the red eye, eh? You look pretty good for a sleep-deprived octogenarian."

"Don't listen to him," Caitlin jumped in, "you don't look a day over seventy-five. Uh, a young seventy-five."

"Morning, Grandma," Jon greeted her with a hug.

Dog house already, and we just got here. "Morning, Dad."

"Mornin'."

"Sleep well in the Brisbane Hilton?" I asked him.

"Is that where we are? It's not my bed, I know that much."

"You guys want to go for breakfast? There's a pancake house just down the highway." And nothing. No reaction from my father. For years he would fume when servers, clerks, anybody said "guys" as if it were genderless. To him it was guys and gals and the universal "guys" was a slap in the face.

"Yes," my mother said, "that would be wonderful. I'd rather delay trying the dining room downstairs until lunch or dinner."

"That's great," my father said, "as long as there's coffee."

65

Caitlin and I drove the point car. Jon drove his grandparents in theirs. And as they say, a grand time was had by all.

As a boy, and as a teenager, I had four sports-related dreams. In baseball: to pitch a perfect game and to hit a grand slam. In golf: to make a hole in one. In bowling: to roll a 300 game. In all but one, I failed. I pitched a no-hitter, but never a perfect game. I did, however, hit a grand slam. In golf I missed a hole in one on a par three golf course outside of Lake George, New York. In bowling my high score was a 238.

My father watched my no hitter pitched in a Little League game when I was 12 years old. I was already five foot nine and a hundred and sixty pounds. On a regulation diamond the distance from the pitcher's rubber to home plate is sixty feet six inches. In Little League the distance is a mere forty-five feet. The point is most Little League pitchers never reach five foot nine at twelve years old, so I had an enormous advantage over hitters because I had an unusually fast fastball. Pitches don't break much in forty-five feet, but a tall kid could launch a mean fastball—especially past nine and ten-year olds. (In the stands for a home game once my mother shushed a stranger when he shouted, "Jesus Christ, when did that kid start to shave?" when I took the mound. "He didn't," my mother informed him.)

But Dad missed my grand slam by five minutes. I was playing Pony League (fourteen to sixteen-year olds). I was pitching the game—on off days I played first or third—so as the pitcher I batted ninth. In the third inning bases were loaded with two out when I came to bat. I fouled the first pitch but caught a solid piece of the next one into the deepest part of left field—barely, but it cleared—like Bill Mazarowski's World Series winning shot in the bottom of the ninth in the seventh game of the 1960 October Classic. I remember watching my hit drop over the fence just out reach of the left fielder's glove. My heart hammered in my chest. I don't remember running the bases. To this day, nothing.

My father was not a golfer. Truth be told, neither was I. I only played, with ancient wooden shaft clubs I bought at a garage sale for five bucks, because caddy day was Tuesdays and we could play the

Country Club course all day for free. At thirteen, fourteen and fifteen I was a caddy—a good, and one of the only jobs available to young teen boys in the sixties—carrying doubles for ten dollars a round, eighteen long holes. Five mile course. Strong like bull.

On vacation my father agreed to play nine holes with me on a gorgeous, hilly course near Lake George, New York. (Dad had great strength, but little finesse. A straight-line, no-hook bowler, he powered through the pins. Twice I saw him break pins at the neck.) In Lake George he crushed his drives the first time he ever held a driver. But his short game took him into double digits on the score card. He didn't fuss and fume. He had no skin in the game. He shot. We walked. He had a ball.

The next day we decided to try a par-three course that was maybe attached to the other course, I don't remember. What I do remember was the tee on hole number one was on a cliff, the green was directly below. Total distance to the pin was maybe five or ten yards, not counting the twenty-foot drop. Dad asked me to club him. I handed him my nine iron. He skied it into the bunker on the far side of the green. "Shit," he said. "Oh, well."

I teed up, made a chip shot to the green where it rolled about a foot and came to a stop at the lip of the hole. I held my breath. So close. So close!

He slapped me on the shoulder, smiling. "We've got eight more holes, right?"

I bowled six strikes in a row to open a game when I was about sixteen. I started to think I might roll that 300. I choked in the seventh frame, barely converting a spare. Then I thought I might match my father's high score of 256, but I lost my rhythm. I struck just two more times and stumbled out of the tenth frame with a 238.

February 2014

Dr. Samuelson called on a Monday morning anxious to have our thoughts about the new treatment option he had reported to us. I told him our concerns, explained that from where we sat "so called" Alzheimer's cures didn't have the greatest success. "I shudder every time I think about those people a few years back."

"That was then," he assured me, "the research has been moving forward by the proverbial leaps and bounds. And no, no one wanted to see a repeat of that hell."

"What kind of guarantee can you give us that when Dad recovers that's it, no returning to the monsters."

"Monsters?"

"Yeah, you know on old maps, unknown or unexplored places were labeled 'there be monsters' or 'there be dragons.' That's where I imagine my father lives most of the time, if not in hell, then in the nightmare next door."

Was that a nervous chuckle? "Jack, you know I can't give you any guarantees, nobody can, but I can tell you I have been watching this treatment very carefully. I have seen nothing so far that raises any kind of red flag, nothing even comes close to alarming me. We always cross our fingers, and toes, but the results at this point have been nothing short of stunning, exactly what we have been seeking for decades."

"You've seen this with your own eyes? Not just studies in *JAMA*?"

"Up close, Jack. I've been eyeball to eyeball with twelve different patients. And they are clear-headed as you and I." That was not as reassuring as, I'm sure, he intended it to be given our family's experiences over the past few years. But I understood the point he was trying to make.

"That's good to know. I'll relay that to Caitlin and Jon."

"Have a family Pow Wow, Jack. Think about how good it would be to hear Warren's voice again. I think you'd even welcome back the old war stories."

"We're thinking about it, all of us, every day. Give us a little more time. Far as I can tell, there are no do-overs with this."

"Okay, Jack. But let me remind you, your Dad's north of ninety and not in the best of health—pneumonia three times in the past two years."

"Believe me, it enters into the equation."

October 2009

Bonnie died in June. My parents stayed in their house until October, then moved to 2B at Brisbane Towers. Before the end of that month the kitchenette began to resemble Mount Avenue, with cereal boxes, cans, jars of kitchen utensils piled up on the counters and the tiny kitchen table that had become, by default, where my father "played with his coins." But he didn't, really. What coins he needed for his collection were forgotten. He took rolls of coins he had opened and rerolled back to the bank to exchange for new rolls. He did this so often he was very likely going through the same rolls two, three, even four times. No wonder he so rarely found a coin he needed, those two forces worked constantly against him, and the bank, of course, could not keep track of what he brought in and what he carried out.

The coins, along with his solitaire cards and Word-Find books kept him occupied for hours, breaking only for the bathroom, meals and sleep. In those quiet hours my mother would read or slip out to go downstairs and chat with her new-found acquaintances. She seemed, if not happy, at least content. At any rate, she did not preface every visit with questions about when they might be going home.

And there was an unexpected, unanticipated and unpredicted consequence of those hours of my father's silence and isolation—the old story-teller began to lose his words. For decades my mother had been filling in blanks in his conversations, completing his sentences. His stories, however, were sacrosanct, they were like, for him, what literary critics call set pieces—battles scenes, pastoral descriptions that can be inserted into a narrative when the plot threads are dropped by the scop or bard momentarily. The story is made to appear seamless by these set pieces that are etched on the story-teller's mind. The audience is none the wiser, a reputation is maintained, and the old familiar story takes on unexpected new lifeblood. *It was different this time*, listeners might say, *better, a little bit unexpected.* Conversations, which are new every time, left Dad grasping for the right words sometimes, and occasionally for any words at all. "It happens to us all," we'd justify to ourselves. But his stories were something different, they were composed, rehearsed and refined over many years. Oh, he would embellish when needed, he always had, also conflate and polish further—all of the alterations any good spinner of tales and yarns makes if only to keep the story fresh for himself.

It began, over the first months at 2B, like the stories, lovingly recorded, had broken and been repaired so that there were holes, odd silences, meaningless juxtapositions of words where others had been cut out. These left his new audience, down stairs in the communal lobby, afternoon and evening gathering place for the denizens (mostly men) of Brisbane Towers, scratching their mostly bald heads both literally and figuratively. For years the receivers of my father's stories would ask," What did Warren mean when he said…?" Now they asked, "What was Warren trying to say?"

Most days he just sat and listened to the Big Band music by Glenn Miller, Harry James and the Dorsey brothers that mysteriously filled the lobby and dining room throughout the waking hours.

*

About the same time we began to notice the serious decay in my father's stories, he also began to arrive back at the apartment, after short trips to the bank or Post Office, with dings, scratches and missing or dangling mirrors on the car.

Driving off and leaving my mother at the Shop Rite had resulted in a brief rescinding of my father's driving privileges. For a few weeks he climbed into the passenger seat when they went out together. He said nothing, seemed to acquiesce, and the tension between husband and wife simmered, then cooled. Before long he was running errands, quick trips to the grocery store, the barber shop, the bank. Occasionally, at first, when my mother was feeling the degradation of yet another chemo treatment, Dad would drive her home, to the hospital or doctor's office. And then, by some sleight of hand none of us could explain, he was back behind the wheel full time, menacing other drivers and, surprisingly, not scaring my mother half to death. The one time I agreed to ride in the back seat, I closed my eyes and resigned myself to the inevitable crash that was surely coming around the next bend or the next corner. During that fright-fest my mother sat stoically in the front passenger's seat, catatonic or blissfully unaware of the close calls they

71

avoided every couple of minutes. It was, at once, a fascinating and terrifying experience, and one that they, my parents, repeated every day.

But now he was no longer just missing the light stanchions, fence posts and garage door frames. The car had received so many small insults that my mother could no longer discern new dents and divots in the doors and quarter panels. It was hard to ignore the majorly mangled mirrors, but for a while, she did, I thought.

"Mom, let's talk about something."

"Uh, oh."

"Not about you. About Dad."

"You've seen the car."

"I have. It's a mess, to say the least."

"I know."

"How long do you think it will be before these one-car mishaps turn into a serious crash, and someone, Dad or somebody else, maybe a child, gets hurt—or worse?"

"Honestly, I'm amazed it hasn't happened already."

With that statement, my anger flared. How could she, he, they be so selfish? I was afraid to open my mouth.

"You're angry," she said. "You've never hidden that well. I know we should have talked about this a long time ago."

"Really? You think?"

"Jack, I can't drive any longer. I've tried. I don't have the arm or wrist strength to drive safely."

"So, Dad drives, and…?"

"And we still get to go to the store, out to lunch—I won't let him drive after dark—to the library. You know?"

"Not to be melodramatic…"

"So, don't be. I don't want to be dismissive, but your father is all we have left of our independence, our freedom, do you understand, Jack?"

"I'm not stupid."

"I know that. Far from it."

Is this little bit of independence worth somebody's life? Seriously, Mom. You remember how mad you were when Dad drove off and left you at Shop Rite. Imagine if he 'forgot' and caused an accident, cut somebody off, ran a red light, and that somebody go hurt really bad. Could you live with that?"

My mother started to cry. Caitlin, quiet until now at the other end of the sofa, gave me the 'end of conversation' look. I opened a magazine and stared at pictures of spring flowers.

We still get to go to the library, out to lunch. Jesus Christ, now I was even angrier at myself, not for wanting them off the roads and safe, but for not thinking hard enough about what ordinary things mean to us all. From the time we're sixteen or seventeen years old, we drive— many of us. It's a rite of passage, as watered down as it is, in our twentieth and twenty first century American world. For many it's the first break from parents. It means freedom, a chance to be with whom we choose rather than with those we're tribed with at birth. The child dies, the adult is born, we hope. Most teens take the responsibility seriously, those who don't sometimes pay the price for refusing to let the child die—metaphorically.

I went for a walk.

One day I arrived at The Towers just as my parents were pulling out of the parking lot. My mother was behind the wheel. The only reason I knew it was them was because of the battered Saturn. My mother looked like an adolescent girl, tiny, intent, barely able to see over the steering wheel. My father, now barely five foot eight, hunkered next to her, nonchalant, lost, I supposed, in some car ride eighty years before, perhaps the one to Asbury Park with his parents and siblings to see the Morro Castle run aground and burning off the coast behind Convention Hall. Or down to Lakehurst to see the wreckage of the Hindenburg. They had watched the flames from the burning blimp from their hill top farm only days before. "Oh, the humanity," they heard on the radio. Theirs was the first generation to grow up in and around automobiles, and even in their eighties they look at home in their beat-up Saturn, aged teens off to yet another adventure.

I carry the image of my mother behind the wheel that day, tiny and consumed by the vehicle's size and relative power. They were going to the store, then to the diner (they forgot I was coming), or maybe just for a ride as they once did a lifetime ago. Just for a ride, to escape the place they had been forced into, away from strangers, institutional food, smells and sounds they would never get used to. I didn't flag them down, or even tell them later that I had been there, I simply watched them drive off. That was theirs, together and separately, to remember or not, but to enjoy for as long as it lasted. Free of me. Free of Bonnie, and Caitlin and Jon. Call it their secret.

The Pablo Neruda poem I had read in college kept running through my head again as I walked around the building looking at the tall trees, old growth undisturbed when they built the apartment block. "I happen to be tired of being a man." And at that moment, for the first time, I thought I understood what he meant. Yes, we were doing the right things to keep my parents safe by moving them to quarters where help was nearby. But God damnit, I never asked to become a parent again in my sixties. To micro-manage my parents' lives, to tell them what they could or couldn't do, where they could or couldn't live, or go on their own. But here it was: Dad, you need to give me your keys. You're not allowed to drive anymore, You, the man who taught *me* to drive—and to throw and catch and hit a baseball, cast a fishing line, shoot a basketball, roll a bowling ball—can no longer pack up your wife and drive to Food Town or Shop Rite for milk and coffee and bread. You must take the bus provided by Bainbridge Towers when they say and to where they are going.

Shit! I wouldn't blame him if he tried to hit me, to hold his keys clutched in his fist and dared me to try and take them away from him. I would not. I would sooner flatten the tires (would he notice?) or disconnect spark plug wires, but I would not disarm him, strip freedom from him as you would a favorite toy from a belligerent, out of control child. I would not reduce him to that. Protect him? You bet, any day of my life, but confront him, control him, insult him—even with the hard truth—no. I would give him wrong keys on the right key chain—his frustrations were real, but fleeting—but I would not do one thing to smudge his dignity, in his eyes or mine.

Drive? I'm sorry. Hell no. Return to Asbury Park? Go! May it be as clear as you remember the blue sky, the smoking ship canted

74

sideways in the surf, the surf itself, the sand and crowds, maybe some popcorn or peanuts on the boardwalk. Take the ride down Ocean Avenue south from Sandy Hook Proving Grounds where you would soon enough serve in the Army, patrol the beach and find, not one, but two floaters washed ashore, to Asbury Park. You are twelve years old again, the resort is bustling, it is alive. It was better then than it is now. Go! See it maybe for the first time—again. Except for the mysterious fire, the 134 people who died, the massive crowds jostling to see the massive ship floundering in the surf, it is a day to remember, a day you remember. Go! Drive? Hell no. It is so much faster and safer to take the memory-train, or better still, your father's Model T, the whole fam-damnly piled inside for the adventure you alone are left to remember.

My father sat at the table he had unknowingly claimed for himself and was so deep in a Word-Find puzzle that he hadn't noticed my mother's crying and laughing or the making of tea. Now, coffee would have jarred him back into this world, but tea had no effect. He just kept on circling, following the method he had perfected and tried to explain to me one time, to no avail.

"Do you have any idea how to approach this?" my mother asked me.

"We could disappear the car in the middle of the night. Take it to our house."

"That would be a lot of trouble, don't you think?"

"Not as much as some other plans I hatched in the last half hour or so."

"I don't want to hear about those."

"I had no intention of telling you, just of acting surprised one day."

"You wouldn't."

"You're right." Caitlin laughed.

"Why don't you do what we did with my father?" she asked.

"Refresh my memory. Oh, never mind, I remember. That might just work."

"Somebody going to fill me in?" my mother asked.

"Well," Caitlin said, "we told my father that because of the gas shortage you could only drive your car every other day."

"What gas shortage?" my mother interrupted.

"Oh, the one in the late seventies."

"But your father died a decade later, right?"

"Yup. He remembered the gas shortage. So, every day we'd tell him that it wasn't his day to drive."

"That's awful," my mother grimaced.

"But humane. It kept him off the roads and we didn't have to stomp all over his dignity to do it."

"How is Dad's memory of the seventies?" I asked.

"Pretty clear. Sometimes he talks about Jon as if he were still a little boy."

"Thank you, dear," I said to my wife, "I think we're going to take out your little ploy and knock the cob webs off of it."

"It's worth a try," my mother said. "I don't want you to have to cut the spark plug wires." We glanced over at my father, his pencil poised above the page, intent on spearing the next breathless word hiding in his jungle of disassociated letters.

Early February 2014

"Let's have dinner," I suggested, "just the three of us, so we can talk about Dr. Samuelson's latest. Have either of you seen anything on the net or on the news about this "cure" he's talking about?"

"No," Jon said, "and the web is usually crawling with rumors and half truths about stuff like that. Ominously quiet."

"Caitlin?"

"Not a word, and honestly, it makes me nervous."

"Amen to that."

"Jon, what are you thinking? It seems to me we have to be unanimous. We're all in or we're all out."

"I agree." Caitlin got up from the table and walked to the kitchen.

"I have to tell you, I feel like my time with grandpa was cut short. It seems like he declined so quickly. One week he's telling stories, the next week he's making that strange cooing sound and all of the people in the day room are also cooing or laughing about it."

"You gotta hand it to him, he's figured out a way to get the last word in."

Caitlin came back and sat down. I just took some pork chops out for dinner and called Dr. Samuelson."

"Really?"

"Um hmm. Yeah, I told him about our concern that none of us could find any information about this cure. I told him I would have expected it to be headline news."

"What did he say?"

"He said it would be—soon. He said the pharmaceutical company that developed the drug was keeping it very quiet."

"Why? It seems to me this is as big a news story as the polio vaccine or the HIV cocktail."

"Almost exactly what I said. He told me the drug company is small, this is the first major drug they're bringing to market. Apparently, they're nervous and don't want to jump the gun. They don't want to be the next breakthrough to backfire."

"It sounds like they're trying to make themselves leak proof. Good luck with that," Jon said.

"What I'm wondering is how Samuelson knows so much. If he knows, don't a lot of docs know too?"

"He's on their board," Caitlin said, "sworn to secrecy. He can't even tell us the name of the company unless he wants to be sued."

"Hmmm. You learned a lot in a short conversation."

"I speak his language, remember? I told him we felt too much in the dark, that we didn't feel comfortable making a decision without more information."

"And he said?"

"Everything I just told you. Pay attention."

"Anyone else feeling uneasy with all the hush hush stuff, Samuelson on the board, freshman venture by a nameless company?" I asked.

"I am now," Jon said.

Caitlin nodded.

"Listen, in my imagination I've had long conversations with grandpa, listened to the war stories like for the first time. I would like nothing better than to have him back, but I remember you talking about what happened a few years back and that's a fresh hell I wouldn't wish on anyone. Do we have a deadline for our decision?"

"Not that I know of," I told him, "but I think these kinds of trials often have a cap on the number of participants just in case something goes haywire. That may be Samuelson's concern, they may be approaching that number."

"Well, I know I'm not comfortable casting a yes vote just yet. Jon?"

"Me either."

"Great."

Caitlin patted my arm. "I'll call Samuelson back tomorrow and see what else I can pry out of him. He seems anxious to get Dad enrolled ASAP. In the meantime, how about some pork chops and Pinot?"

"Sorry, Mom. Gotta fly. I have a date."

October/November 2009

We, Caitlin, Jon and I, started to anticipate a relatively peaceful Thanksgiving like the ones we all looked forward to twenty/thirty years ago. I told my parents one of us would pick them up and drive them to our house where they could stay as long as they liked. "No, no," Dad complained. "We'll drive up ourselves."

"We will in a pig's eye," my mother shot back. "They offered to pick us up and we're going to take them up on it."

"Okay," Dad finally consented, "but I'll drive home." Right! That speed bump crossed, Caitlin and I began to discuss the menu. We each remembered different dishes from our childhoods—I fondly recalled green bean casserole (abandoned in recent years due to the excessive fat content) Caitlin said her family used to have apple dumplings—whether that was a nod to the autumnal harvest or the German genes, I didn't know. We decided both dishes would offer a little nostalgia—good memories—in an otherwise painful season.

Jon vaguely and not fondly remembered his great grandmother one year made giblet gravy and giblet stuffing. He asked us nicely if we would please, Please! Leave both dishes off of the nostalgia menu. "I can still taste the iron on my tongue." Consider it done and done, we assured him in unison and harmony like half a barbershop quartet. No sweetbreads. Promise.

My mother offered to make the pearl onions in sauce my father liked so much, and which neither Caitlin nor I had ever learned to make. It seemed a job just about the right size for her reduced kitchen, so we agreed.

There is a turkey farm about six miles from our house, so on a Saturday morning about three weeks before Thanksgiving, Caitlin and I drove there and placed our order for a twenty-pound bird. That done, and the rest of the day unspoken for we decided to drive down to our old stomping grounds and maybe cut some mountain laurel and white pine for a Thanksgiving Day centerpiece. Laurel, though illegal to harvest, grew in abundance and we could access the woods through Bayside cemetery.

"We can cut some greens then drive down Ocean Avenue to Sea Bright or Long Branch and stop for lunch."

"Sounds like a plan," Caitlin said.

To my surprise, and hers, the day went exactly as we had planned. We had both lived in Long Branch when we were younger, before we met, and we both recalled a street where there were three Italian restaurants—Nunzio's, Tuzio's, and a third we could never remember the name of so dubbed it Threezio's. We picked Nunzio's where we shared a large Philly cheese steak and a very cold bottle of Cavit Pinot Grigio.

We spent the whole afternoon without once talking about Bonnie or my parents' ailments. We knew it was going to be a tough holiday but celebrating it at our house rather than at the old homestead we hoped would make it easier on all of us. We decided to invite some friends as well. That distraction, along with the cooking and bartending would keep us too busy to think about the previous ten months—like I said, we hoped.

Jon was going to bring his new girlfriend—bingo! one more thing to keep us blissfully distracted. Nothing like having to behave for strangers.

On the ride home Caitlin fell asleep. The smell of white pine and two plus glasses of white wine were too much, I guess. So, for a little more than an hour I drove, only WNEW AM out of New York playing almost inaudibly in the background, the skeletons of oaks and maples and poplars standing sentinel beside the highway. Had I not heard a weather forecast earlier in the day, I would have sworn the sky was threatening an unusually early autumn snow.

*

Caitlin woke as we pulled into the driveway. "Welcome back," I said.

"Thank you," she mumbled, "for not waking me. I dreamed the whole time I was in some cartoonish Christmas village, world, I don't know. There were no elves, and strangely no kids."

81

"Not allowed," I offered, "Santa knows if they spend too much time in a place where it's presents and reindeer and happiness all the time they get sensory overload. May never look forward to Christmas again. A big hazard in the Christmas village trade."

"Nice theory, Sigmund. Wasn't it the good doctor who said that sometimes a cigar is just a cigar?"

"Yup. Sorry for clogging all over your dream of Christmas never. It was probably lunchtime and the kids were on break."

"That's better. What time is it?"

"About seven."

"That all? That was a quick trip. So how fast were you going?"

"In order: Yup. Surprisingly little traffic. Speed limit, more or less."

Inside, I glanced at the phone. "Missed Calls" flashed slowly on the little screen. I picked up the handset and clicked through the day's calls: Caitlin's brother, Ken; a colleague; a bogus threat from the 'IRS'; my parents. "Your brother called," I shouted to Caitlin, "and my parents."

What did they have to say?"

"Who?"

"Any of them."

"I haven't listened to the messages yet." I listened. "Ken called to say hello and that he hadn't heard from you, us, in a while."

"And your parents? Come on, Jack. Get with the program, will you."

"Mom said to call her."

"Uh, oh."

"I'll call." The phone rang eight times before Mom picked up.

'Hello, Jack, your father fell this afternoon. I called you hours ago. Where have you been?"

"Ordering a turkey, but more importantly, how is Dad?"

"Nothing broken, but he's got an egg on his head where it hit the table. I called, and two nurses came and got him off the floor and into bed."

"Did they suspect he had a concussion?"

"Apparently not, but they told me to keep an eye on him, try to keep him quiet and awake for a few hours. I'm to call them at nine tonight."

"Jesus, Mom, how did he fall?"

"I put my crochet bag under his table out of the way. Somehow, when he stood up, his feet got tangled in the straps and down he went."

I cupped my hand over the mouthpiece and said to Caitlin, "Dad fell."

"Oh, no. Is he all right?"

I nodded yes.

"Do we need to come down there?"

"I don't think so, Jack. The nurses are two minutes away. If anything comes up, they can handle it."

"You sure?"

"Yes, I've been sitting in the rocking chair in the bedroom crocheting and trying to keep him talking. He gets annoyed with me, but he quiets down pretty quick."

"How about if I come down tomorrow for a few hours. We could go for a ride if you like. Are there any stores you need to go to?"

"Don't cancel any classes on our account."

"Tomorrow's Sunday."

"Oh. Let me think about your store idea. I might need yarn, and it would be good to see something other than these four walls. And plan to stay for lunch or dinner in the dining room. There are a few people I'd like you to meet."

"It's a date. I'll call you when I get on the road."

"Call my cell. I might be downstairs kibitzing. Be careful."

"I will. Love you, Mom. Good night."

"What happened?" Caitlin asked.

November 2009

When Bonnie died, my father still had his fingernails dug into the world the rest of us recognized and identified as being a part of. But that world, for him, was crumbling—fast. Now, only five months later only one hand was still holding on. At dinner on Sunday my mother introduced me to some of her new acquaintances; my father, on the other hand…

"I'd like you to meet my father," he said to a man who eyed me suspiciously.

"Your father, Warren? Really?"

"Oh, for crying out loud," he said lightly slapping his forehead with his palm. "I meant my brother." This was the first time I experienced his total lack of recognition, and it shocked and frightened me. We knew it was coming, but no one is ever ready, not really. He smiled at me, "Isn't that right?" he asked.

"No," I told him, "I'm your son."

"That's what I said."

"No, Warren, you said he was your father, then your brother."

Dad looked at me and narrowed his eyes. I knew that look, he was silently asking me if I too recognized that this man was off the wall. He cocked his head, "If you say so." He turned and walked away. Click.

Dinner went smoothly, more or less. Instead of entertaining between bites with anecdotes and scenes from sixty years ago, he concentrated on his food. With each bite he would raise his head and look around the room, but apparently not seeing anyone. He never nodded to waves from the next table, never smiled at the hands placed on his shoulder by people passing by. He gave no hint that he understood there was anyone else in the world.

Back in 2B, my father went to the bathroom, I said to my mother, "that was weird."

"What was? Dinner?"

"No, no, before dinner. Dad introduced me as his father, then as his brother. When the man questioned him, Dad dismissed the guy with an eye roll and that look of his that says, "this guy's nuts.""

My mother was crocheting. She stopped. "His father?"

"Yup, father, head smack, brother. Does he do that to you?"

"No, well a few times he's forgotten my name. He forgets. You know, there's a lot of stuff stored up there in his eighty-eight years," she said, looking to do some damage control.

"How long? How come I haven't seen this before?"

"You have. He covers. Have you noticed he rarely calls you, any of us, by name anymore? Rather than stumble or wait for me to fill in the blanks, he just skips that part. Jack," she started to cry, "I lost my daughter, and now I'm losing my best friend. I don't know what to do. I know this sounds selfish, but I just can't take care of him any longer, my own health …well, you know."

Rarely in my life have I felt speechless, but this was one of them. I sat down on the sofa next to my mother and hugged her thin, unfamiliar self. Oddly, what ran through my mind in that instant was my mother would have killed to be that thin after two kids. She was never heavy, but that never mattered.

My father returned to the living room and smiled. "What are you two cooking up, Jack?"

The garden was maybe twelve feet wide by thirty feet long. In it, when I was a boy, were dahlias whose blooms were the size of dinner plates and whose stalks were as thick as a man's wrist. And the colors, oh, my god, yellows, reds, oranges, purples, pinks. But those names don't do them justice. Sunlight, blood, pumpkin, plum, watermelon flesh. But…no.

All winter the bulbs languished in our basement in bushel and peach baskets smelling of earth. Brown, misshapen hands of roots; some vaguely doll shaped; others looked like carrots or potatoes or the dirigibles that floated overhead on languid summer afternoons, appearing out of nowhere, disappearing like skeins of geese into the blue distance on their way, perhaps, to dock at the Empire State Building. All winter I found excuses to escape into the cellar to hold them in my hands, sniff the dirt that clung to them promising spring and their annual burial. Even as a very little boy I realized that placing them in a grave-like hole in the ground meant flowers, meant giant, colorful blossoms and a playground. They grew maybe four feet tall— taller than me, much taller—on sturdy stalks that I could crawl amongst for hours pushing just my imagination ahead of me. Too young to go down the street to the woods to play, the garden became my woods, a magic place that smelled in summer like the cellar in winter—and years later like the local greenhouses I visited in snow time just to bury hands up to my wrists in fragrant dirt. This was after my father lost his passion for the gorgeous dahlia blooms and turned instead to heirloom tomatoes, green beans, kohlrabi—long before every garden catalog listed umpteen varieties of each. Where he found them, I don't know. I suspect he collected them as he had collected new colors of dahlias, by trading with friends who shared his enthusiasm.

Some of my father's passions were quixotic—he was half way through his decade long love affair with dahlias when I was born. He stuck with vegetables twice that amount of time. What he lacked in duration, he made up for in depth. In the last years of dahlia mania my father knew more about that variety of flower than perhaps all but the most ardent Ph.D. in botany.

In high school my father taught ballroom dancing. He started the club, held dances, taught the fox trot and waltz. He worked at the local hardware store where records—78's—were sold. He was responsible for keeping up with what was spinning on the airwaves and making sure the bins were filled with the fat black platters of Miller, James, and Patti Page. His master plan, as I have come to sus it out, was to keep on teaching dance after graduation. Had it not been for the inconvenience of the War, he might have managed a career at Arthur Murray dance studios. Might have one day owned a franchise. But the war...

So, he channeled his energy—too much, my mother would attest— into dahlias, his boy scout troop, politics, then into his children. I was the recipient of his largesse—of his flowers, his vegetables, his antiques. Even in a bass ackwards way his coin collecting in that I grew to despise the gathering of too many like things. I burned my matchbook collection as soon as I was old enough to strike one of those treasured firesticks.

March 2014

"So, would it be possible to meet one of the patients in the trial?"

Dr. Samuelson did not answer. I began to think I had asked a forbidden question.

"You want us to commit my father to an unproven treatment?"

"It's working, Jack. Remember that," he interrupted.

"I think we have every right to explore, on our own, what's happening with the people already being treated."

"I know, I know, Jack. But I'm not sure the company will greenlight a visit. They're new to this. They don't want to screw it up."

"I get it. We're new to this too. I understand what you're saying, but we're not going to turn my father into a guinea pig just because you've had six months of success, that could, as we well know, go south at any time."

"Point taken," he said. "Let me run this by them and I'll get back to you. Everyone else jumped at this. This is a new wrinkle."

"With all due respect, we almost went down this alley once before." Silence. "Try to understand where we're coming from. I would trade my eye teeth to hear the old stories, the same old, same old. I could even forget I've heard it all a hundred times before. But..."

"An abundance of caution, I get it."

Do you? Ninety-one years! He's living fifty, sixty, seventy or maybe more years in the past, and he's happy."

"Jack, I'll do what I can to set up a visit. The company will have to okay it, the family, the patient will have to be onboard. It could take time. Maybe time we don't have."

"This is twice you've brought up the obvious in conversations. Is there something we don't know about? We'll let you do what you need to do but let me lay this out for both of us. You want us to agree to bring my father back into a world, his world, that has changed unimaginably—his daughter is dead, his wife is dead, his home for the past sixty five years is gone, he is living in a nursing home—a place he expressly said he did not want to ever live in—among complete strangers, for all intents and purposes people he has never met. For the past few years he has not known me, Caitlin, Jon. He is living in, I don't know, depends on the day, the thirties, maybe, the forties, fifties, sixties? How long have those other people been gone? What is the fog they inhabit, inhabited, pardon me? What in Christ's name might a shock like that do to him? Couldn't the cure be worse than the disease? Do you understand my concerns?"

"Thank you."

"For what?" I snapped.

"I guess a different perspective. I've been so excited to see the disease reversed I hadn't thought about the other consequences. Let me look into this a little more."

"We'd love to meet some of these people," I said.

"Sure, I'll get back to you."

"Thank you. Just so you understand, I miss my father. I know, he's still here physically, that's not what I meant. I want him back, but at the same time I don't want to be selfish. He's been through enough. Maybe being stuck in a time when you were supremely happy isn't so bad."

"Maybe it isn't."

November 2009

I told Caitlin what my mother said about not being able to care for my father any longer. "She's bone weary, and she's starting to collect and read all sorts of quasi-religious books. My mother is terrified of dying, and I think she's caught a glimpse of something."

"Like?"

"I don't know. She's different. I don't know if it's this whole thing with my father that's changed her, or maybe it's the cancer, or the chemo, or all of it. Her health has always been ify, compromised to one degree or another, so I don't know how she's held up this long. Maybe she should have skipped the purgatory of 2B and gone straight into a nursing home."

"I think she needed these months out of her environment, all the memories, the sadness of the last few years, and maybe get used to the inevitable."

"I don't know—I say that a lot lately, huh? —but it's true. That Sunday we had dinner."

"Last week."

"Really? Well, after Dad went to bed, we talked. She proposed going home. Just her. 'All I'd need would be a bed and a chair down stairs. A television, a snack table. I'd be happy, I'd be all right,' she told me. And she's serious."

"She knows Dad needs to be under twenty-four-hour care. Do you think she would consider a nursing home for rehab, a few months to see how it might work out?"

"Honestly? No, I don't."

"Me either, but we have to do something before there's another crisis, emergency. I don't even want to think about what might happen next."

"Will you go with me to talk with her? Maybe Jon, too. I don't want her to think we're ganging up on her, but she'll shoot me down before hearing me out."

"Of course I'll go with you."

"Can you work your magic again, do some research so we have answers to her objections?"

"Sure thing, just say the word."

"Word," I said.

"I'm on it."

"We never think it will come to this, do we?"

"No, we hope it will never come to this."

It's horrible to say, but my father was going to be the easy one despite his lifetime resistance to ever, ever going into a nursing home. Both of his parents died at home, and that's where he would die as well. But we were already once removed from that possibility and growing more distant every day.

My mother, on the other hand, was much sicker than he, but still had control of her faculties. My father, alone, among siblings, parents, grandparents and extended family had developed dementia. My mother's family doppelganger was cancer in all, it seemed from a distance, of its awful and painful manifestations. No one had avoided it, no one.

I refused to ever think about the double whammy I might face down the road. We needed to spend energy on heading off the next crisis now.

We never made it to Thanksgiving. We put the turkey in the freezer, called and apologized to our friends for the last-minute cancellation, then Caitlin began a whirlwind search for a nursing home.

The week before Thanksgiving I accompanied my mother to her oncologist's appointment for the first time. Normally my mother would drive herself and my father to the office, then out to the diner, then home—a marathon that exhausted them both for the next two days. Her visit struck me as a typical physician's visit—for someone in good health. Beyond the pleasantries, the vital signs and several general health questions, there was nothing that suggested the patient was in stage four cancer—begun in the ovaries (*mostly* removed decades earlier) and now metastasized to bone and beyond.

When we got up to leave, the doctor motioned for me to remain behind. I did, and Mom walked out to the waiting room on the arm of a nurse. I had seen this movie before.

"Dr. Wilson," she began. The address caught me up short. I am a doctor, Ph.D., not a medical doctor and outside of academia I'm rarely addressed as doctor. It's not on our mailbox or in the phone book. "Your mother talks about you a lot," she said.

"Oh," I said, "I wondered because I'm not wearing the hat today."

Chuckle. "Listen, I know you and your wife moved your parents out of their home a few months ago, a wise choice, I think."

"Dr. Abernathy, it wasn't a choice, it was a necessity."

"I stand corrected. My point is, even a smaller, one-floor apartment with nursing assistance on site is no longer sufficient support for your mother—and father. Your mother is very frail, and when I saw your father last week, well, I'd say he's declining very quickly. Do you agree?"

"Reluctantly, but yes, I do. What are you suggesting?"

"We're beyond assisted living. They both need around-the-clock monitoring."

"A nursing home."

"I can recommend some good ones."

"That's going to be a hard sell. My maternal grandmother died in a nursing home that was a nightmare of a place."

"How many years ago?"

"Let's see, almost thirty."

"Nursing homes were primitive then compared to what they are today. Seriously, no comparison. I suggest you visit a few. Those with availability are always happy to give you the tour."

"We'll do that."

"I'm sorry, nobody wants to go into a nursing home, and nobody wants to send their parents to one."

At this point in the conversation I had all but stopped listening. The subject had been broached, the recommendation proffered. The rest was just the expected social noise. I was already driving the car, my mother's eyes drilling holes in the side of my head.

"Have a nice chat with Dr. Abernathy, Jack?" she would ask.

"Yes, I did."

"And?" she'd ask.

The question, and its answer, hung as heavy as the Liberty Bell in Independence Hall in Philadelphia she had taken Bonnie and me to see when we were kids. *Odd metaphor*, I thought. *But then again not, her liberty, her independence hung in the balance.*

I did not want to put her in the car or take that ride more than anything I had not wanted to do ever in my life.

"And?" she insisted, settling into the passenger's seat.

"What do you think she wanted to talk to me about?"

"Has it shown up somewhere else?"

"Dr. Abernathy would have told you that herself if it had. She's not one to pawn off the tough stuff on others. She gave you your first diagnosis, she told you when it metastasized to the bone. No, that's not what she wanted to talk about." I started the car.

"What then?"

I took a deep breath. "Housing. Your living situation. A nursing home," I finally blurted. She clammed up and glared out through the windshield, then not another word all the way back to 2B. When we reached the parking lot, she opened the car door, climbed out, and slammed it as hard as she was able. When I opened my door, she finally said, "Don't bother. I'll tell your father you said goodbye." And that was that. She turned and walked to the building and did not look

94

back. It was the angriest she had ever been with me, and the nursing home had not even been my idea.

That was a Thursday. On Saturday Caitlin, Jon and I toured three of the nursing homes on the Doctor's list ranging from the Spartan to the posh. "So, where are your parents living now, they each asked as we rode an elevator to the second or third floor or peered into a day room busy with card games, coloring, ball tossing and here and there conversation groups. In one of those busy rooms I thought I heard Eddie Cantor's "Josephine Please Don't Lean on the Bell" playing softly in the background.

The Alzheimer's units were a different story. There were far fewer activities, and many more one-on-one interactions between residents and staff members, and the air was a strange blend of Mr. Clean and ammonia, urine ammonia, Clorox and feces. Someone was constantly mopping floors or scrubbing the tables. I could not imagine my father placed in such a situation. I felt sick to my stomach. *Why can't we come up with an alternative to this?* Jon saw my face. "Hey, Dad. Let's go for a walk outside. Let's see what the grounds look like."

While Jon and I walked, Caitlin gathered information and said our thank you's. My heart was pounding when we got back in the car. I handed the keys to Caitlin. "You drive."

"The Alzheimer's unit is like what I imagine prison to be, something out of 'Scared Straight,'" Jon said. I stared straight ahead and kept quiet.

"It has to be heavily monitored," Caitlin offered, "if someone took off...well, there's a highway right outside the front door. Talk about the makings of a nightmare."

"If my father could have seen, even a couple of years ago, what his future looked like he'd have found a way...Not living, existing," I said to myself out loud.

"But it's not five years, or even two years ago, Dad. It's now. For us it's a horror, but for Grandpa it may as well be the Plaza."

I shot Jon a look. "Sorry, Dad."

95

"Jon's right, Jack. For all we know Dad spends his days, and maybe his nights, on a troopship in the Southwest Pacific, 1944."

"Or maybe he's back on the farm burying Model T's."

"It's Grandma I worry about the most. She'll know where she is and who put her there. Grandma and Grandpa used to have an album that they played sometimes by that guy, the comedian who's been in so much trouble lately."

"Bill Cosby?"

"Yeah. I remember a routine where he made the observation that the best thing about dementia was you'd never know you have it."

*

Before going home, we swung by Mount Avenue to make sure everything was secure, plus I wanted to get a sense of how many dumpsters we were going to need to clear out the rest of the house after the estate sale. While Caitlin checked doors and windows, Jon and I climbed into the attic; it was a far cry from the empty space containing the darkroom and some boxes of Christmas decorations I remembered from my childhood.

"We could have roller skated up here when I was a kid," I told Jon.

"How?"

"It wasn't packed floor to ceiling like it is now. Now we can barely walk."

"Now we can barely climb over. What are you going to do with all this stuff? I know they liked to collect, but this looks like a hoarder's heaven."

"Oh, just wait. There's a reason you weren't allowed beyond the living area of the house."

We moved downstairs to the bedrooms. Everything was buttoned up tight, beds neatly made, closets partially cleaned out. Nothing dripped in the bathroom. Outside of Bonnie's old bedroom Jon stopped. He cracked the door and looked inside. It was the room that had been the nursery for me, for Bonnie, then it became her room for years. Finally, it was the room my father quietly moved into after sixty years of sharing quarters with my mother. It had lost all signs of babies and girls. It was stark, almost military like. A photograph of my father's Army unit hung over the headboard, some numismatic books and magazines stood slanted sideways on the built-in bookshelves. Jon closed the door. "I miss aunt Bonnie, ya know? Damnit."

We moved downstairs, then to the basement. Again, we could barely move. As children we had roller skated on the concrete floor on rainy days. Now it was a storage unit with a little breathing room between boxes, bags, furniture, anything that no longer could be squeezed into living room, dining room or kitchen. Stuff seemed like it flowed, lava-like, down the stairs from the first and second floors to the dark place where Dad rested his dahlia bulbs during the winter so many years ago. Instead of the intoxicating scent of dirt in February, I smelled the faint odor of damp cardboard.

The oil burning furnace divided the space. Where there had been a coal bin and my father's work bench—appropriated in my adolescence for my "chemistry lab" was now piles of things even I didn't recognize. Jon closed his eyes and shook his head. "Really?"

"Really," I said.

We moved on to the garage, a building not original to the property, but was added in the mid-sixties to accommodate two cars—which it did for a decade or so. At some point my father added an eight by eight greenhouse to the side of the garage to start tomatoes, peppers, eggplant and squash in early March. By then the dahlias were history along with the darkroom high above us.

Now both the garage and the greenhouse were literally stuffed to the point where doors had to be muscled shut. When I opened the garage side door, Jon said, "I'm not going in there."

"Why?" I laughed.

"Could be an avalanche."

"Good point. Seen enough?"

"It's an eye opener. All this stuff hiding in plain sight my whole life."

"What do you think, a thirty-yard dumpster?"

"Then some."

"How much some?"

"Two, maybe three thirties."

"Let's hope the estate sale cleans out a bunch."

"That's a king-sized hope, Dad."

That evening I called my mother to say we'd like to come by on Sunday to talk to her about a few things. She answered coldly.

"So, this is it? You want to talk about a nursing home even though you know full well it's in our living wills that we do not want to go there—ever, Jack?"

"I know. Let's talk about it tomorrow. Just sleep on it."

"Fat chance of that happening. Have a good night, son."

"That went well," I said to Caitlin after hanging up. "Gird your loins tomorrow, I'm warning you, she's going to be out for both of us."

"I'm already girded and I'm polishing my shield."

"Okay, let's talk about the places we looked at today. Which one did you like—if 'like' is the right word?"

"Umm, I guess the one I hated the least was Tall Pines, that two-story number at the edge of what used to be a forest. I liked the staff, it was clean. You want some wine?"

"Yes, please. A pint."

"What flavor?" she asked, standing up.

"Color, flavor, make and model don't matter."

"Coming up."

"While Caitlin opened bottles in the kitchen, the doubts came in and sat down next to me. *What the hell are we about to do?* I must have said my thoughts out loud because Caitlin answered me.

"We're about to save two people we all love very much. Forget your mother's anger, it'll pass. I don't care how many nurses are only two minutes from their door, one of them is going to get hurt. Not might, they are going to."

"Do you think they'll ever forgive us?"

"I don't know. I hope so. But I'd rather go to my grave knowing they were angry—but cared for, looked after in a way we can't at this point in our lives—than be sorry we honored a wish recorded long before anyone could have predicted their health today. How about you?"

"I agree. But that doesn't make it any easier. My mother is going to pull out all the stops tomorrow. Any signs of my weakening kick me in the shins or hit me in the head with something solid."

"Happy to oblige. Promise you'll do the same."

I nodded and gave her a fake grin before knocking back half of my glass of Pinot Grigio. "Tall Pines is what we propose."

"Right."

"Now, how do we approach the estate sale and clean out?"

Caitlin sipped her wine then looked at me with that sad look you give a three-year-old who's just asked, in all sincerity, why he can't put his finger in the dog's nose. Her eyes closed, and she shook her head very slowly, glad, I suspect, she was not the woman who raised me. "We don't," she said softly, "not now."

As it turned out, it was I who couldn't sleep that night. Every time I started to doze, another image from one of the Alzheimer's unit day rooms reappeared: a lady rocking and cooing to a doll; a man holding an animated discussion with an empty chair; another lady whose lips were mashed shut violently shook her head every time an aid tried to feed her a porridge-like bite of food. Every image forced me, no matter how hard I tried to reject it, to imagine my father just like those people. *And how soon?* I kept asking myself. *A couple of months? a couple of years?* I confronted the pictures in my head as long as I could stand it. I got quietly out of bed and walked out to the living room. I stirred up the embers in the wood stove, then fed it a wad of old news and a fresh log. In a few minutes it was blazing.

I sat in my recliner and turned on the television. Reruns and infomercials—what an obnoxious portmanteau word that is—yesterday's news and weather, which, until cable, had been given five minutes of air time twice a day. If you wanted to know the weather, you looked out the window. Emergency-worthy weather drew an extended blast from the firehouse siren. Now the same snowflake fell a thousand times, the same lightning bolt struck the same tree until it was imprinted on your brain—even with your eyes closed.

I shut it off, poured some Merlot and grabbed my dog-eared copy of Joseph Campbell's *Myths to Live By*. I sipped and nibbled on his prose, small bites of big ideas. The memories of the nursing home visits crawled back into whatever void disturbing images live in.

I woke with a start when Caitlin lightly touched my shoulder. "Jesus," I sputtered.

"How long you been out here?"

"What time is it?"

"Almost five."

"Then, umm, I did some quick math with my finger on the fog hanging over my brain, "about four hours." I looked over at my wine glass, it was nearly empty. "I must have just fallen asleep. I might as well just stay up now," I said.

"You do that, I'll see you back here in about two hours. In the meantime, make yourself useful," she yawned, "empty the dishwasher, fold the laundry." Caitlin smiled and went back to bed. I drained my glass and stared at the blank tv screen. I wondered if Dad's dreams had changed. I wondered if Alzheimer's disease, or any dementia, short circuited the subconscious or the unconscious. I made a mental note to ask Dr. Samuelson the next time I talked to him—if he even knew.

I stood up and got my sea legs, then headed in the general direction of the kitchen and the laundry room waiting to see which spirit moved me first: the squeakiness of clean dishes, or the spring-rain scent of clothes spun dry in the night. Either chore would keep me from thinking about what we were facing later—I hoped, but probably not. A faint smell-memory of ammonia and Clorox was already swimming around in my brain.

My mother was stoic when she met us at the door to 2B. She hugged Jon and Caitlin, then turned and walked back to the sofa. "Hi, Dad," I said. He was seated at the little table with a Word-Find book open in front of him. He raised his hand in a wave but didn't speak. "Okay," I said under my breath.

Mom sat primly on the couch. She was wearing a skirt—unusual for her in the past few decades—and a sweater. She had tucked a tissue into the cuff of the left sleeve. It was what her mother had done for as long as I knew her—maybe for her whole life.

"Before you say anything, Jack, tell me exactly what you and Dr. Abernathy talked about the other day." Her voice was not angry and mechanical, as I had expected. It was soft, not in the least confrontational.

"She told me that the last time you and Dad were together in her office that Dad appeared to have," I dropped my voice out of respect, "declined…a great deal. She was concerned for both of you. She remembered thinking that if Dad ever needed to be physically helped— say if he fell—you could never help him, that you might actually hurt yourself if you tried."

She nodded. I took a deep breath.

"She also said you were the frailest she had ever seen you. She's afraid the chemo might be doing more harm than good. Sorry." I was looking at my mother, but I could not look her in the eye. Just as no parent should ever have to bury a child, no child should ever have to have this conversation with their parent. The balance was off. I held my breath. I knew how she was feeling, kind of, but I didn't know how she would react.

Instead of speaking, my mother stood up from the sofa and walked over to my father. She took his hand. "Warren. Warren, come with me." They walked back and sat together holding hands. "I know this has to be very hard on you, Jack. I'm sorry. And thank you for being the one to talk to me. I love Dr. Abernathy, but she is not my daughter, my blood. I'm proud of all of you…." She looked at Catlin and Jon, then looked me straight in the eye, "for keeping us all together over the past few months. I don't know if I could have done it if I were in your place."

For the first time since Bonnie's death, I hung my head and allowed the tears to come.

Dad stayed on the sofa as long as he could manage, then he got up and went back to the table, his safe place in a world that had become muted colors, blurred edges and meaningless sounds. I envied him, that moment, his tiny sanctuary.

"Where are we going?" my mother asked, "and when?"

Caitlin fielded the question. "We looked at three places yesterday. The one we thought you would like is called Tall Pines."

"The building backs on a forest. There are nice views from most of the windows," Jon offered.

"Will you come to see us?"

"Don't we always?" I asked. "You won't be prisoners. We can go out to dinner or go shopping if you're up to it."

"I can't take care of your father anymore, Jack. I realized that last night. I can barely take care of myself."

"You will have separate rooms, on separate wings. But you can be together whenever you want."

She smiled. "That's good."

Late February 2014

We met Dr. Samuelson on a cold and breezy Wednesday afternoon at two o'clock. We sat in our car until he pulled to the curb behind us. We got out and greeted him with handshakes. He seemed distracted, nervous, or perhaps, both.

"This is a first," he told us, "I didn't really think the company would let anyone meet one of their patients, but they agreed with a single provision."

"Uh oh," Caitlin said, "does it involve a first-born child?"

For the first time ever, I heard the doctor laugh. "That's pretty funny," he said to her.

"I'm serious," she said, no hint of a smile.

"Really?" His face fell.

"No, of course not. I'm just trying to lighten things up. We're both really nervous."

"Oh," he smiled again. Well, don't be. But after this interview you need to keep the patient's identity and location to yourselves. Talk about the visit but keep the identifying specifics between the two of you. Okay?"

"Absolutely."

"Mr. Powers is excited to talk to you. He reminds me a little of your father, or at least the Warren you've told me about. A Talker. Stories? He's got a million of them."

"Well, I've been a listener all my life. Had to be in our house. Dad rarely shut up. Mom used to say you had to be a lumberjack—just to drive a word in wedge-wise."

"Then get ready, his twin brother's just inside that door. He prefers to be called Phil. He's eighty-three, his wife's name is Nancy, also

103

eighty-three. Ready?" Nathan Samuelson knocked on the door and Nancy Powers opened it as if she had been standing there waiting."

"Come in," she said with a wide smile, "my name is Nancy and my husband, Phil, is in the parlor, follow me, please." It was a large, new house, open floor plan, hardwood floors, neutral paint on the walls. As promised, Phil was sitting watching a tennis match on t.v. But as soon as we walked in, he shut it off. Doctor Samuelson made the formal introductions. "Sit anywhere," the Powers told us. We sat side by side on a love seat. Silence. No one seemed to know how or where to begin.

"I've already told Phil and Nancy about your father," the doctor said.

"You must have a thousand questions, so fire away, I'm rearing to talk."

"How would you describe how you felt, before, in the, I call it the fog, but I'm just guessing," I said.

"Sure," Phil nodded, "fog pretty well describes it. Yeah, but also constantly being disoriented. Listen, have you ever hiked or camped in the Pine Barrens?"

"We have."

"Good. Do you know the dwarf forest?"

"Heard of it, never been there. Sorry."

"No, no, let me tell you, it's a strange place. A variety of pine tree grows there that has been burned so often by forest fires its cones have evolved to shoot out seeds as soon as the fire goes out. Seedlings appear within a few days. The reason I'm telling you this is the trees only grow to about this height—another adaptation," he said holding his hand five and half or six feet off the floor. "Dozens of hikers get lost in that forest every year and rangers have to go in there and guide them out. See, the hikers fail to orient to the sun, and there's nothing else to orient to, no bull pines, or high ground—nothing. And that's how I felt, except there were no rangers to save me." He stopped. Worry came over his face. "I don't want to frighten you, you know. It could be very different for him. Who knows, when you're in it, the fog as you call it, or the dwarf forest, you can't tell anyone what it's like. In the end it steals your words."

"You're trapped?" Caitlin asked him. We all knew the answer before he nodded to her.

"Like someone in a coma. You're aware but can't move. With Alzheimer's it's your voice, not your body. Your speech signals get all tangled up." He looked at Doctor Samuelson.

"I've heard that same analogy from others."

"Day after day," Phil continued, "you wake up in a strange land and you don't speak the language. Everyone treats you nicely, but they treat you like…a child, a very young child. It was maddening." He glanced at Dr. Samuelson, who blushed.

Nancy asked if anyone would care for coffee, tea or soda. Phil asked for tea with lemon, something he had never cared for before. The rest of us declined. Nancy patted her husband on the shoulder as she passed him on her way to the kitchen. There was a wonderful tenderness in her expression, and I thought I saw not a little relief as well.

My brief experience with the disease had shown me that the pressure is off the victim and everything ever expected of them was transferred to the caregiver who also had to continue fulfilling their own obligations, and meeting people's expectations of them. A double whammy, if you will. It's why caretakers who have brief, or no, relief burn out so fast. It's non-stop, twenty-four-hour attention and worry about falling, choking and wandering off. The challenge of interpreting the patient's non-verbal clues and demands sends the best and strongest, the most well-meaning helper into health spirals they often can't pull out of. My mother, I realized too late, had probably sacrificed months, maybe years of her own life until the very last moment and agreed to enter the nursing home to save them both even though she knew she would, and did, despise every single moment she was there.

It wasn't just Phil who got a reprieve to tell his stories again and spread the survivor's gospel, Nancy had received one too. We could not but feel happy for them.

"You like tennis?" Phil asked during a lull in the conversation.

Caitlin shook her head. "Baseball's more my game," I said.

"Too pastoral, too slow."

"If we ask anything too personal, just let us know," Caitlin said.

"Sure. What would you like to know?"

"I don't know the right words to ask my next question," she said. "How long…"

"How long was I 'in the fog' to use Jack's terms? The last thing I mostly remember was moving into this house after the other one burned to the ground, December 2009. Four years? Threefour years Nancy and Dr. Samuelson tell me. Could have been a day or a decade. 'Time doesn't mean nor matter' one of the other patients said to me. Caitlin, time doesn't exist in the fog, except what it keeps doing to your body."

"May I quote you on that, Phil?" Dr. Samuelson joked.

"I'm oft quoted, doc. Feel free."

"Were there any major changes in your life during that three or four years?" I asked. "Death of people close to you specifically?"

"None that I know of, unless Nancy is keeping something from me. She's healthy, the kids and grands are fine. Far away, but fine."

"Have they come to see you?" I asked.

"One of the first things I remember was seeing my granddaughter's face. I called her by name. She told me, 'Pop Pop, you haven't known me since I was in the fourth grade, now I'm in middle school.' Hard to admit to folks I just met, but that made me cry."

Nancy returned with Phil's tea. He looked tired. He had told us a lot in the past two hours, much more than he thought he had. We thanked them both and left.

"Thank you," I said shaking Dr. Samuelson's hand, "for going out on a limb for us. His identity is safe with us. We have a lot to chew on. We'll be in touch soon."

My paternal grandparents owned a farm, a small one, five or six acres, on a place called Chapel Hill, New Jersey. This was land the Wilson's had purchased in the mid-eighteenth century. The original farm was roughly one hundred acres, but it had been parceled out over the centuries to brothers and sisters, cousins and "relatives" who did

not occupy limbs or branches on the family tree, but mere twigs. What remained in the possession of my immediate line was a fragment of the original purchase. But my grandfather was proud to own the largest remaining tract which he subdivided into plots for tomatoes, cucumbers, corn, peppers, cantaloupes, squash, and at the back of the field, potatoes and sweet potatoes. For years I walked up the hill in the summer to help my grandfather hoe or pick or flip the sweet potato vines every few days to keep the crop cool.

He had an old Fordson tractor that he used to plow the field each spring. Then, gathering as many of the tribe as he could, we would plant. I was often assigned, as the oldest grandchild, the plot behind the garage where cucumbers were the designated crop. And for years every spring I would pull car parts out of the furrows—old fashioned head light, steering wheels, wheel rims. Every Spring I made a pile, and then the pile was gone. I thought of it as the car garden.

One day on his way home from work my father stopped at the farm just as I was tossing yet another headlight on the dirt-encrusted pile mounting at the back of the garage. "Know what that is?" he asked me, no doubt seeing the puzzled look on my face.

"I think so, but why are all of these car parts here, but not anywhere else in the field.?"

"You want a story? Or the story?"

"The story, I guess."

"Okay. Back in the 1920's your grandfather worked for the Carhart and Gilmore estates as a caretaker. He cut the grass, trimmed hedges, pulled weeds in the gardens."

"I thought he was the caretaker of Bayside Cemetery?"

"He did that too."

"So, these were rich people?"

"Oh, you bet. Old money, and they weren't afraid to spend it. They had maids, cooks, caretakers like your grandfather. Hard to believe, but every year they bought new Model T's for everyone in the family. The old ones were in perfectly fine shape, but they had to have the newest—even though every year looked the same. At some point Mr. Carhart, or Mr. Gilmore, maybe both, I can't remember, asked my *father if he would like to have last year's cars. Really? He said to them. Take them, they said. So, every day he drove one home. In a couple of years, he had quite a collection. But when he tried to sell them, then give them away, nobody would take them."*

"Why? I would have."

"Me too, but nobody he knew could afford the gas. So, each year there were two or even three or four more cars parked behind the garage. Then at some point, when I was very young, my mother had had enough of the used car lot growing in her driveway. I'm guessing here, but my father was probably given an order to get rid of the T's. Like I said, few people had money to keep them on the road."

"But grand dad did?"

"He was always working at something, so he usually had a few dollars. Anyway, so my brother, my father and I, just like the pond we dug behind the cemetery, we dug a grave for the model T's. It took us weeks. Dug a huge hole—not very deep, but really long and wide— deep enough to cover the cars. Out of sight, out of mind, they say. My mother was satisfied. The cars were as good as gone—planted, so to speak, buried, whatever. That's when my father began to refer to his farm as Peaceful Valley—despite the fact that they were on the very summit of Chapel Hill."

"Really?" I asked him, suspecting this was a story, not the story as promised.

"Yeah, really," he said. "Where do you think all those nuts and bolts and steering wheels come from? Care to dig down three or four feet and see if you run into a hood or a frame?"

"No," I said. My father shrugged. Click.

Mid December 2009

Six months after Bonnie died, and three months after moving into 2B at Brisbane Towers, my parents were taken by ambulance to Tall Pines nursing home—my mother to Spruce wing, an ambulatory unit, my father to Juniper, the Alzheimer's floor. Mom was relieved, but monumentally unhappy and even more so when a staff member recommended hospice. She was furious and refused, in no uncertain terms. "I'm not *that* sick," she informed the hospice representative.

We visited every few days, and each time my mother asked me if I thought she could go home now that Dad was safely being cared for. I told her we could talk about it after she'd had time to rest up and get to know the place. "I have no interest whatsoever in knowing this place. None. It would be much more restful in my own bed, in the house I've lived in for sixty-five years, Jack. I read an article that said people are healthier and happier in familiar surroundings. Look around," she whispered, "most of these people are very, very sick. I'll probably catch something. And soon. At home . . ."

"Yeah . . .You could fall, you could be on the floor for days and nobody would know. You've seen the commercials on T.V. right? Or you could choke."

"I'm not a choker, never have been. So, you can cross that off of your little list."

"Bad example," I said.

"So why can't I go home?"

I wanted to avoid pointing out the obvious, but it was all I had left. Logic and reason weren't working. What she wanted was a fantasy. I could understand how she felt, I could understand someone whose whole world was coming unglued at virtually every joint could convince themselves that home would heal them, it was the place that for over six decades had indeed healed every one of us in her family at some point or another. She, of course, overlooked Bonnie, Dad, her own illness. But I couldn't.

"Mom, look," I said, "even if I thought that your going home was a good idea, which I don't, you wouldn't be alone in the house two hours before one of your doctors would call Adult Protective Services and have you taken into custody, and then God knows where they might place you. It surely wouldn't be here with Dad."

She stared at me until it was just plain uncomfortable. I stood up and walked to the window. "The last thing I want to be in your eyes is the bad guy, but if that is the way it has to be, so be it. I have and will keep on making decisions that keep you safe."

"I want to rest my eyes for a little while, son. Will you still be here?"

"I'll go visit with Dad. You rest, I'll be back."

My father and I talked for about an hour. Well, mostly I talked, and he sometimes listened. We sat in a common area between their two wings. Oddly, he didn't seem to notice that Mom wasn't with us. I eventually took him back to Juniper and went to see my mother before I left to go home.

Back in her room she was just waking up. "Jack," she said, "I was just thinking, maybe we wouldn't need to tell the doctors."

I blew out a frustrated breath. "Nice try, Mom. What would you tell the nursing home, you were going on a world cruise and you'll be back in a couple of years? You're in the system now, and the system, like it or not, is keeping its eye on you."

"Well, I don't like it, Jack, not even a little bit."

"You're not alone. Most people don't like it until they fall through the cracks, get lost or forgotten. You become a non-entity, a number, if you're lucky enough to retain that much identity. If not, poof, it's like you never existed at all."

"Maybe that's not as bad as you make it sound."

"Really? What has kept you alive for the last five years, your house? your husband? your children? A little bit of all that, I grant you, but only a little. The biggest chunk was the system—your surgeries, your tests, medications, doctors, nurses—a whole complex of people and smaller systems within the larger one, so many pieces you and I, and maybe even your doctors don't know that much about. Is that fail-safe you are now a part of what you want to try and hide from?"

"Yes."

"What? Why?"

"We're not systems people, Jack. No clubs, no organizations, boards, associations. I've never been attracted to groups."

"Well, Dad was, the fire company, library association, local government, boy scouts, you name it."

"Think about what you're saying. When was the last time your father went to a meeting—and I don't mean to talk to high school students about the War? He hasn't been a boy scout leader in almost half a century. He quit the fire company when the younger members wouldn't even try to remember his name. That was forty, forty-five years ago. The young Warren Wilson was a joiner. No more."

"I'm not a joiner either, Mom."

"I know, I know."

"I don't have any memberships beyond National Geographic. I only attend faculty meetings because I have to. Outside of the classroom I don't like large gatherings of people."

"That's my point."

"But I'm part of the system. I have bank accounts, I have a cell phone, I use utilities, I have a wallet full of credit cards and I pay their balances every month on the internet. I'm plugged in, you're plugged in just by being alive. It's damned hard to disconnect or avoid being connected in the first place. The system is harder to avoid than it is to accept it is a side effect of being a modern-day human being. 'Tune in, turn on, drop out,' isn't that what Timothy Leary was saying in the sixties? Remember? But you can't drop out anymore. The sixties were the dark ages compared to today. The system may be a safety net or a spider's web, but it's got us one way or the other. At some point we blinked, Mom, all of us and flew right into the sticky threads."

"Oh, Jack, enough. Enough, enough, enough. You wear me down and you wear me out. The parent becomes the child, I get it. Thank you for protecting us, especially your father."

"Don't."

"Don't what? Don't thank you? Don't appreciate? Don't keep trying to get back home? What?"

"I'm simply doing what I watched you do when Me Mom got sick, couldn't stay at home any longer. I watched the toll it took on you. I watched you struggle with what you knew you had to do. I understood that no one else could just jump in, it was all on you, and you did what had to be done. Now it's my turn."

"This will be my, our, first Christmas away from the house since 1945."

"I know."

"I wonder what they do around here."

"I'm sure they try to make it as festive as possible. After all, every staff member has to be away from their home too—for a while. And they're already putting up decorations, there's a big tree in the second-floor common area, a cut tree, a fir, I think. And there's also a huge menorah."

"I saw that, I forgot what it was called. I love the holidays."

"You may be the all-time champ. How many Santa Claus figures do you have now?"

"Pssh, I lost count years ago," she laughed, "there got to be so many we had to leave them out all year. Your father refused to haul them up and down the attic stairs any more. But there are some still in the attic that just come out after Thanksgiving. Jack, do you remember when you were a boy we used to decorate my parents' tree, right about this time of the month, then we'd decorate ours on Christmas Eve? Then it evolved into a party." My mother went silent, lost, I presumed, remembering the smoked whiting we only bought during the holidays, the fried chicken, cold cuts, hard rolls from the Downtown Bakery, Me Mom's potato salad, Mom's own baked beans all laid out buffet style, and then there were the Grasshoppers my father concocted in the blender and my grandmother insisted could not possibly have any alcohol in them. Hiccup. Click.

"Mom?"

"Jack?"

"What if we had Christmas at your house this year? Like we used to, decorate a tree Christmas Eve, sandwiches, chicken, the whole spread?"

"Can you get us out of here?"

"We got you in, we can get you out."

"Over night? I'd love to wake up in the house on Christmas morning."

"I'll see what I can do. No promises, okay?"

"Yes." I handed her a small victory. "I can't wait to tell your father."

"Let's wait on that a few days. Let's surprise him."

"Good idea," she winked. "No presents, you understand. This will be our present this year."

"We'll see. Where's the tree?"

"In the basement, I think. But it doesn't matter. The ornaments are in the attic. Oh, I know, let's do a Snoopy tree, wait 'til Christmas Eve and buy the scraggliest one no one else wants."

"But you always like to have a big, full Douglas fir."

"Yeah. I know. And I always wanted to live to be a hundred." My mother was suddenly happy.

On December 23 Jon and I huddled and laid out a plan for Christmas Eve. Between us we could pick up food, people, Crème de Menthe and a forsaken Christmas tree on a lot about to close. "I wish we had done this when I was a kid," Jon said, "this is more fun than getting presents."

"It'll be the last Christmas in the house, you know."

"I know. But we'll all remember it."

"That we will. Do you want to split up the tasks now or rendezvous tomorrow and set out from the house?"

"If we set out at the same time, we'll get back about the same time, right?"

"Let's hope. Then we can set out together to find a tree."

"Where do we look?"

I laughed. When I was younger than you I waited until the last minute, bought a tree for two bucks from a guy trying to cut his losses. They were sorry, spare and misshapen. It's a wonder anyone cut them in the first place. But it was fun, I always felt like I was saving the runt of the litter."

"And Grandma and Grandpa always had a big, full tree loaded with ornaments—and a pickle."

"And a house full of Santa Clauses. I guess their maximalism made me a minimalist. Did I ever tell you I collected matchbooks as a kid?"

"No. Well maybe a few hundred times."

"Okay, smartass, then you get to pick up the smoked fish. I hate smoked fish, fisheries. You go. Whiting or ling, whatever. I already reserved two at Elroy's fish smokehouse from hell."

At 2:30 Christmas Eve we deployed to Elroy's, the Shop Rite deli counter, Top–Flight fried chicken, the Downtown Bakery, Uptown Liquors for Crème de Menthe and two or three flavors of wine. At home Caitlin doctored a couple of cans of baked beans as per Mom's recipe and ushered a dozen eggs from carton to deviledness.

By four the refrigerator was bulging. By five Jon had delivered my parents home and he and I left to find a tree. "Let's take Grandpa," Jon said.

I hesitated. "Oh, what the hell. He probably won't get the joke but what the hell. When your mother and I were first married he used to go with me to the woods to cut a tree down—I liked stealing more than buying. And who was going to miss one tree, an absentee landlord? He always drove the get-away car. I jumped out at dusk, slipped into the woods with a saw, cut down the tree we'd scoped out weeks before. Then he'd circle back, stop, help me tie it to the roof, then speed off— as fast as a V.W. bug could speed. One year we found a bird's nest in the tree we cut."

"Let's do that," Jon said.

"Umm, let's not. We could go to jail for that now. Let's just go and find a Snoopy tree and call it Christmas."

But most tree lots were closed. Jon and I looked at one another. "I know where there used to be one," my father said from the back seat.

"Point me," I told him.

"In Buttermilk Valley. There's an old barn."

"I know it."

They were just killing the lights when we pulled up. Half a dozen sorry looking trees leaned against a rope perimeter.

"Not much left to choose from," said the proprietor as we tumbled out of the car.

"That's okay," I said. "We want a bedraggled one."

"Like this?" he asked hauling a godforsaken spruce up on its one leg.

"Exactly," Jon said.

"Four dollars," my father said.

"Fair enough," the man said, "I was going to give it to you, but I'll take your four bucks."

"Thank you," I said digging some bills out of my pocket.

He looked at my father. "Weren't you Mr. Wilson? I was in your Boy Scout troop." He smiled and waved off my money. "Nice to see you."

*

Bonnie never married. Bonnie had no children. Jon had no children, but his new girlfriend, Alexis, had a ten-year-old daughter named Jordon. And all of them came for Christmas Eve. My mother was thrilled, a child in the house. Someone to hide the pickle for, even if there wasn't a present for the one who found it. Since the tree was, to say the least, meager, Jordon found the pickle right away. Jon handed her a chicken leg—we were making it up as we went along. Jordon played along.

Except for the Christmas tree, the living room was as my parents left it before the move to 2B. Mom settled into her chair as if she had never left with an audible sigh of contentment. Dad instantly adopted Jordon and began telling her stories—about the house, about the dahlia bulbs he used to store in the basement each winter, about the tomatoes he grew, and the photographs that once bloomed out of pans of reeking chemicals in the attic darkroom. I watched her. She listened and smiled in all the right places. She was, I thought, enchanted. The old man still had it, the old power to lure a listener into his world. At the same time, she wrapped Dad around her finger, the granddaughter he never had, and likely never would.

As Christmas Eve turned to early Christmas day, Jon took Alexis and Jordon home. We put my parents to bed after a couple of Grasshoppers. I have a form of paradoxical insomnia, I think—where I swear I don't sleep, but actually I do. I must have had it even when I was a kid. On Christmas mornings I was always amazed that Santa Claus had slipped into the house despite my wakeful vigilance. But there was the proof of magic, a pile of presents deposited in the living room under and around the tree. The whole North Pole crew had come and gone right beneath my nose.

We packed up the leftovers in the refrigerator. What Jon and Alexis didn't take, we bagged for tomorrow's lunch. All that was left was to wait for Santa Claus.

Caitlin and I crashed on the sofa like a couple of homeless people happy to find a soft surface to sleep on.

As always, the worst part was the hangover. December 26 meant, at the very least, returning my parents to the nursing home—about as easy as managing a bag full of ferrets. One or the other found a reason to do this or that—the mirror in the bathroom was crooked; the coffee table, hmmm…

We spent an hour straightening chairs, adjusting pictures, putting a life in order. "What about the Christmas tree, Jack? Shouldn't we take it down and put the ornaments back in the attic?" Stalling.

"We'll come back and do it next week."

"Perhaps we could help. Things have their places."

Caitlin and I sat back and watched as my parents staged their rooms. When everything was just so, we locked the door and drove back to Tall Pines.

January-February 2010

Toward the middle of the month we received a letter from Social Security telling us we had to liquidate my parents' assets to pay Tall Pines, etc. etc. It was the worst time of year for an estate sale, but we had no choice. At the same time, real estate taxes were coming due—again—not a small consideration in Central New Jersey, an area that had come to be known as the Wealth Belt. When my parents bought their home post War (1946), that part of New Jersey was just becoming a parking lot for New York City. Now it was a Riviera for rock stars and Wall Street types and taxes soared to nine thousand dollars a year on a quarter acre. We had no choice but to sell.

We hired an estate sale consultant, an expert to help us lay out "the good stuff." We kept as much of this as possible from my mother. On my days off and weekends we picked through and assembled what we thought was the best stuff in their collections. I had no clue. Once I gave up collecting matchbook covers, I began collecting books, but I also quit thinking about the value of stuff. I knew my parents' collections of art glass were substantial, but I had no idea of their worth and now we had no time to have it appraised and offered at auction. We had to trust the dowdy matron we hired as the show runner and her vast expertise in all things antique and collectible. "Hurry up," was the watchword.

We spent all of our time away from work combing through boxes, bags, barrels, crates and drawers trying to find anything that screamed "expensive," important or rare. We had little to go on. An English tea caddy we might have let go for ten dollars eventually went for seventeen hundred at auction. It was 18th Century. Hmm. Maybe she did know shit from shinola. Who knew? A keen eye saved us on that one. Many things I found intriguing were merely intriguing to me, common items, dime-a-dozen. I was completely out of my element. My parents clearly knew their stuff, and at the same time bought the chaff. Much I recognized, but most was strange to me, acquired in buying trips to Pennsylvania and upstate New York, New England, then wrapped in brown paper and stored away.

A few of their collections, Fairy Lamps and Francisware had been written up in regional antique's publications and we expected them to sell high. But season and market said otherwise. On the day of the estate sale it threatened to snow all day. A few bids were called in, but much of the collections was sold to curiosity seekers late in the day to keep the whole sale from being an utter loss. The collection of salts walked off in twos and threes, the courting lamps went not as a lot but one at a time. Clarks sold indiscriminately alongside Fenton-ware lamps. The Francisware sold as it had been acquired, one piece at a time—pitchers, celery jars, toothpick holders.

Caitlin and I chose not to attend, to receive the bad news at the end of the day. What my parents had assembled and had assumed would be their retirement account, was, in a single day, broken into valueless units and let go to buyers who did not know or care what they were buying other than a pretty piece of glass or pewter, woodwork to liven up a drab household. In short, their decades of work amounted to nothing more than an assemblage of stuff for an outsized garage sale. Antiques sold for pennies on the dollar. The estate sale manager, it turns out, knew no more than we did—the tea caddy was a happy accident, a fluke—about what things were worth, and nothing sold for anything like what it was worth.

When she waved a seventeen hundred dollar check in our faces at the end of the day, I wanted to puke. I estimated fifty thousand dollars' worth of antiques and collectibles (but what the hell do I know) had sold for a pittance and a hundred times that much had not sold at all and would be carted off, at great expense, in the next few weeks.

Retirement account gutted. We invited the neighbors, who had steered clear of the sale out of respect, to pick over what remained. Click!

*

We calculated that less than one percent of the contents of the house sold at the Estate sale. Emboldened, we attacked the other ninety nine percent, and quickly realized that two sixty-year-olds and a thirty something son could not rummage through and dislodge sixty-five years' worth of stuff, haul it down from, out of and up from the various hiding places in the house and out-buildings.

We rented a thirty-yard dumpster and four men who gathered every morning on a town street corner hoping to be chosen for day work—lawn-mowing, weeding, painting, job-site cleanup—at twelve bucks an hour. We set them to work on the attic. Like a string of worker ants, they hauled down boxes of Christmas decorations, clothes, books and God-only-knows what all. For two hours they trundled boxes down the rickety stairs and piled them into the dumpster. By ten a.m. that dumpster was packed full. We called the rental company to pick it up and deliver a second one. By eleven they began on the basement. Just as boxes etc. had come down the stairs, now boxes flowed up the narrow stairs out of the dark filled with . . . at some point while I was not watching, my 1949 Lionel trains, my matchbook collection (surprise!), my chemistry lab, to say nothing of the odd assortment of square nails my father had accumulated from some hobby or other disappeared into dumpster three or four.

The hired hands did not pass judgement, they simply carried box after box after box to the dumpster, stacked them, returned, then did it all again hour after hour and dumpster after dumpster—one, two, three—on and on. At the end of a twelve-hour day seven dumpsters had appeared and disappeared from the driveway, all full to bursting, all filled with a life.

From time to time Caitlin or I would spot something familiar in the hands of a stranger and rescue it, an embroidered table cloth, some leather-bound books, photographs—hell, I wanted to salvage it all, wrap it up neatly into a package and place it in a safety-deposit box for a thousand years as if saving stuff might bring Bonnie back, might erase...

It was an assembly line, box after box—down then up, then garage and greenhouse—went to the cold, empty dumpster space, brick on brick unbuilding a home and a life. The mechanicalness of it all was like an anesthesia. There was not an iota, a glance, a moment of emotion. It was simply twelve-dollar-an-hour relentless unpacking and stacking and stacking and stacking. Empty one space, fill up another, tit for tat, this for that. We knew the house weighed heavy on the earth, may have even tilted the compass. That was the old joke. The reality was no joke. Sixty-five years was leaching away, piling into metal boxes that would be lifted to flatbeds and hauled away to . . .

At eight a.m. I was all business. At nine a.m. I was becoming numb, I blanked my mind to what was happening. I went blind to one, two, three, four lives marching into oblivion. Stuff is the people it touched—once upon a time if a pig-bone touched the finger-bone of a saint, that bone—lamb, pig or chicken—was deemed as saintly as the finger-bone. A kind of guilt by association; holiness earned by merely rubbing shoulders. So here I went, the only one of the four lives alive or in attendance, piece by piece to the landfill—or more likely a second-hand shop by way of an attendant flat-bed driver who caught wind by dumpster number three of what was happening at the Wilson abode.

At the end of a very long day the house was empty except for some furniture, some yard decorations, and the few things we had flagged as they were carried past us. The "save" pile was miniscule, the rooms echoed. It was scary-empty. How would I explain this to my mother?

After we added up dumpster and day-labor costs we didn't even break even on the estate sale. Someone, I suspect, realized a big pay day, but it wasn't us. The house lay empty. I sat in Dad's chair, Caitlin and Jon sat on the sofa drained and too exhausted to order a pizza. We paid the workmen one hundred and eighty dollars each and drove them back to the corner where we had picked them up as if that was where they lived. They'd worked hard, eaten the subs we bought at noon, drank cokes and bottled water we kept on ice. They were happy. We were sad. So it goes. So it went.

We were, how you say? bereft. I wanted to curl up, fetus-like and sleep for twenty-four hours, no, years. I wanted my trains back that I'd hoped would surface from the basement jumble, but they slipped away while I was supervising the removal of bags of hammers, boxes of flags and banners, the stuff of knee-jerk, giddy, auction excursions you box up and relegate to dark corners hoping to forget. There were so many boxes, so many regrets—I hoped.

I went back to work on Monday following the clean-out of the house. Caitlin had contacted a realtor who promised to appraise the house and get back to us by the next week then get the house on the market. The township was on our backs, threatening to foreclose if taxes were not paid. We put the For Sale sign out. We dug into our savings and forestalled foreclosure and crossed our fingers.

On February fifth my mother's nurse called me on my cell phone in the middle of a class. "Dr. Wilson, your mother is, well, declining. I'm not sure what's happening, but she is in and out of consciousness."

"Should I come?"

"I don't know."

"Is it urgent? Should I come to the nursing home? In your professional opinion." I knew the nurse by her voice. She was young, and I tried not to sound impatient.

"Umm, I would say yes. This might be . . ."

"I'm on the way." I hung up, dismissed my class without explanation. I had packed a bag weeks ago with clothes, toiletries and whatnot. I was ready. I called Caitlin, then Jon.

Mom was awake when I arrived but could not make herself understood. I think, now, she was asking, "am I dying?" but I couldn't understand her—or didn't want to, but I understood perfectly the look of terror in her eyes. The nurse pulled me into the hallway. "What's happening?" I asked her.

She shook her head. "This one's on you, I'm afraid." She walked away. On me? I went back in the room and held my mother's hand. She was cold and shaking and slowly drifting back into unconsciousness. The same nurse brought my father to the room.

"She's sleeping," he said, then sat down and laid out a hand of solitaire at her bed side. Twice he looked up and offered to wake my mother up. "After you travelled so far, she should at least talk to you."

"It's okay. She needs her sleep. We'll visit when she wakes up."

"All right then." Click.

The nurses finally took Dad back to the Juniper wing. I stayed another hour holding my mother's hand. Jon came and spelled me just as it started to snow. I remembered my mother told me it had snowed, then rained the morning I was born, an Easter Monday. I went out for a sandwich, ate half, got the other half to go.

"I'm going to find a liquor store and a motel room," I told Jon.

"I'm just going to head home."

"Fine. I'll call you."

I gave the charge nurse my cell phone number. "If there are any changes, please call me."

"I will."

I settled in to a Days Inn, poured a glass of Merlot, called Caitlin and turned on MSNBC, "The Rachel Maddow Show," I think, a re-broadcast from earlier in the evening. Threefour glasses later I nodded off. I slept sitting up in my jeans and T-shirt in a chair.

My phone rang at six a.m. My mother had died at three. No call. No warning. No good bye except for my last words, "see you tomorrow, Mom." The hearse was already in transit. No tomorrow. The cancer had won, or the chemo. I poured myself two fingers of vodka, dialed Caitlin, and cried.

I was glad she never had to see the house as empty as the day she took possession, a war bride, months after my father sailed home from the Philippines, nineteen years old and waiting for me to come into their lives. But I was a few years away—stubborn, or reluctant.

I arrived at Tall Pines on the morning of the funeral with a new white shirt, a new tie, new shoes for Dad. His clothes had disappeared in the clean out. Anything he hadn't taken to 2B was gone, so Jon and I went shopping. I have to admit, he cleaned up pretty well, but it was awkward, no, down-right disconcerting, at the very least, helping my father into his pants, buttoning his shirt, tying his shoes. I hadn't realized the extent to which his small-motor skills had declined. I had brought an extra top-coat for him—it was a bitterly cold day with plenty of that snow left on the ground—a little big in the shoulders, but who was going to pay attention? The real question of the day was, did he understand what was happening? He never shed a tear. Only six months before he had wept after the nurse asked him if he knew what had happened to Bonnie.

Enough snow had been moved to allow chairs at the grave side. I didn't know until later that many people had stood in snow up to their ankles. I read a few poems by Seamus Heaney about the death of his mother, held it together long enough to get through the service. The funeral director delivered a serviceable quasi-religious mini-sermon. I toughed through my eulogy and a few more poems. It was a simple ceremony. My folks were not religious, so we left it at that. No church service, just a brief gathering in the cemetery. Simple, my folks would have been happy with simple. For all of her elaborate collections, she preferred a rather stripped-down presentation of her things.

Dad fidgeted throughout, for all the years he had spent in that cemetery he seemed not to recognize it at all, not even the Wilson plot, ours since the Great Depression when the Cemetery Association could not afford to pay my grandfather for his caretaker work, so gave him a fifty by fifty foot burial plot (twenty or twenty-five graves) on a hillside under some old-growth maples. He squirmed. What was going on? His eyes asked. Where he had always greeted people at interment services, he was absent in all but body. I took over, slid into the role easily—I had been paying attention to protocol since I was ten. Unknowingly, that day I also slid into another role, that of clan elder, decision-maker, since my father was no longer available. Chiefly by proxy, I'd say, if anybody inquired. But no one ever did.

We gathered at the Pancake House after the burial since the house was mostly empty and we couldn't expect elderly people to just stand around and eat off of paper plates. We had a brunch in the banquet room. Since we did not have a viewing, we brought a few of the smaller arrangements and placed them discreetly around the room. Family and what few friends remained. My mother would have liked it like this. Simple. Despite the proliferation of collections, she liked clean, shaker-like lines, she liked things gathered in neat, uncomplicated groups. This is what she would have planned if she had planned to die.

Dad didn't know anyone and just wanted to go. Where? It didn't matter. He wanted to go away, back to the familiar, whatever that was for him now. This fuss and bother absolutely unnerved him, and even before the ham and pancakes, the eggs and coffee, Jon offered to drive him back to Tall Pines and help him settle down. Dad wanted his sweat pants and polo shirt, his Velcro-strapped sneakers, and a room where he could sit by himself and visit with whatever memory chose to visit him.

Alzheimer's had erased my mother and sixty-five years of married life together. Today would end with a beach ball being punched and batted around a day room by strangers whose only connection was the room they were forced to gather in together every day.

Before the collecting madness began to fill every living and non-living space with stuff, there was the attic, a large open space on the third floor that, when I was very young, had only a cedar chest and a pile of cardboard boxes containing Christmas decorations. At the front of the house the attic had been sub-divided by my father into a room where he could go and practice magic. At least it seemed like magic to me. It was a darkroom lit, most of the time, by just a small red lightbulb, and stinking of developer and fixer.

My father and my maternal grandfather (his darkroom was in his cellar) took up photography between the end of the war and my birth. Eventually they turned their hobby into a cottage industry. Beginning around Thanksgiving each year for about a decade they would begin booking photography sessions in people's homes. Sometimes they photographed only children, sometimes the whole family—unlike today, cats and dog were not included in family portraits. They would shoot rolls of film, take them home, develop them—this is where the magic happened when blank white photo paper went into the developer where it slowly bloomed with faces and hands and bodies—slide them into a fixer bath, then clothespin them to a line to dry. Then these were taken, a few days later, back to the clients who would choose the shot that would become their Christmas card.

When it was too cold to paint houses after his day job, my father would ascend the rickety stairs to the attic and spend hours at the work benches he had built along two walls developing and printing roll after roll of 35-millimeter film all by the glow of that puny red light.

`On the benches were white enameled pans, gallon jugs of developer and fixer, stacks of photographic paper, various tongs, scissors, a magnifying glass and jeweler's loop, and a two-inch by three-inch framed nude, who I learned years later was Marilyn Monroe. It puzzled me that my mother, who often worked side by side with my father in the darkroom, didn't seem to mind that the picture

125

was there, or maybe she did and was simply honoring his space. It was never mentioned, at least not around me.

Whenever Bonnie and I were going to the attic with our parents, we were advised to hit the bathroom first because once the darkroom door was closed and the lights, except for the red one, were turned off, the door could not be opened without spoiling every picture that was in the process of becoming. And sometimes that could be hours.

I never got the chance to develop a photo I had taken. One Hour, inexpensive photo developing shops brought an end to the need for home darkrooms just about the time my father lost his enthusiasm for snapping pictures—that and the Polaroid. The darkroom was gradually abandoned, and that magical space quickly filled up with junk—a true anti-magic.

June 2012

After the master story-teller could no longer tell his stories, he began to make a peculiar cooing sound. It erupted out of him and woke up the day room. "Coo-coo," it began. "Coo," someone in a far corner replied. "Coo-coo," another resident responded, then an aid took up the call. Two or three more residents joined the choir.

"Coo-coo," my father could no longer tell his tales, but he found a way to reach an audience. "Coo-coo," he said, and they sang back, laughing, "Coo-coo." A bird song, a nonsensical, joyful, desperate utterance from someplace deep inside and so scrambled that one syllable was all he could muster. "Coo-coo," over and over, the day room erupted, call and response, residents and aids, nurses and janitors cooing this nonsense song until Juniper was laughing. Dad, a nurse told me, exhaled and smiled. Click!

And it was not an isolated incident. It happened time and time again. Sometimes "Coo," sometimes "Caw," and sometimes "Whoop." Whatever was going on in his confused brain, something told him, 'make 'em laugh. Even if they're baffled, make 'em laugh.' And day after day, they told me, he made them laugh, a miracle, once again, a photograph blooming out of developer. Magician. Father. Trickster, maker of life and light.

February 2014

Dr. Samuelson called on the third. Phil Powers had died of a heart attack, completely unrelated to his Alzheimer's treatment.

Caitlin called Nancy, but the widow had little to say, barely remembering our visit. We called the Valley Florist and had flowers sent to the funeral home. Habits.

I called him back on the seventh and left a message. We had been impressed with Phil, enjoyed talking with him and Nancy. But I wanted more. As I always told my students, one is unique, two is coincidence, but three is a pattern. Phil's stories had delighted us, but now we wanted to talk to a coincidence, and then, to screw the lid on our decision, I wanted to talk to a pattern-maker.

An hour later he called me back. I thought I heard a bit of irritation in his voice. *Tough shit. This is my father. Good for your patients who had emerged and thrived, but I want context.* Phil had told us there had been no major changes in his life. He went away, and came home to the same house, the same front door, the same paint on the shingles, the same family.

It was not the same circumstances for my father and I wanted to talk to someone who returned to a world that had changed, changed utterly.

"I don't know everyone's situation, Jack. There are nearly fifty people involved. Some I know, some I've never met. I'll ask around and see if there's anyone who fits the bill, whose case is more like Warren's, okay?"

"Case?"

"That's semantics, Jack"

"No, it's Warren Wilson, Nathan. My father. I don't give a good god-damn about your study, trial, experiment, whatever name you want to give it— "call it '*Awakening*'—but we are not going to do something without shining a light into every alley way and every possible bad ending that we can think of. Coming out of the fog is not the be all and end all in itself."

The line went silent. I thought I heard him thinking—far, far away. Tick, tick, tick.

"I'm sorry, okay? I'm running on adrenaline. No trial or study or drug has ever achieved this much sustained success. I guess I'm so close to this that I get flummoxed by anyone who doesn't seem to want to be a part of it."

"We want to be part of it, but we don't want your success to become the very thing that creates an unexpected, unanticipated hell for my father. To see him lucid again would be the best outcome we could hope for—but at what expense? Can you tell me that? What would it cost him to find himself in yet another world he did not recognize, and also couldn't escape. We're well aware of the daily confusion, you've made that part very clear to us. We get it. But what if clarity is worse? What if his new reality is something he can't deal with all at once, and there would be no way to stop *that* all at once. No going back. It would hit him—hard and fast."

God-damn, Jack. God-damn you. I was, we were, riding this high, so many happy people." Silence. "I'll call you back."

I hung up. "Samuelson's pissed at us, at me."

"So what? They're like a bunch of kids with a chemistry set."

"A big, fat dangerous chemistry set."

"Right. They haven't thunk it through. A quick success and they think it's all the same for every patient. But it never will be. Before this gets out of hand they need to slow down. No one's saying that this isn't a potentially century-shaping deal, but they need to think how many ways that deal could be shaped."

I wanted Phil and Nancy's son and daughter to be more like us, maybe have answers we could contemplate. Sure, I wanted to ask my father if he remembered the day I hit a grand slam only minutes before he made it to the field, if he remembered the night he rolled his 256, or the evening his ice-cream cone money went to replace a burned-out headlight. But I didn't want to ask him if he knew, if he recalled that his only daughter was dead from a car accident, or that his wife of six plus decades had finally lost her lonely fight with metastatic ovarian cancer.

Spring 2012

Tuesdays or Thursdays each week, my non-teaching/office days, I reserved for visiting with my father, though by this time he did not know who Caitlin and Jon were, and only occasionally did he remember me. Earlier in the year he had begun aspirating his food at times and eventually it led to pneumonia and a stay in the hospital. In three or four days he was back in the Tall Pines—but without his dentures, the hospital had "misplaced" them and all he could do was gum solid food. So, after consulting with the staff nutritionist it was decided to put Dad on a soft food diet—mashed potatoes, mashed cauliflower, chicken puree, etc. Now, my father, at least in his adult years, was never a small man—his Army uniform pants had been a '30 waist, but he had been a 38-40 inch since the 1970's. The pulverized diet, I was assured, would revert back to solid food as soon as the hospital replaced the "misplaced" teeth. We waited a year. By that time, he refused to wear the new dentures, they hurt him, and he had become used to the near-liquid diet. My father had already shrunk from six feet to five foot eight, and now he was losing weight as well. A once robust 200-pound man was shrinking before our eyes. The monthly medical reports following my mother's death listed his weight as 197 in January when he entered Tall Pines, to one hundred ninety pounds in March 2010, one hundred eighty-five in April, and so on down and down. By 2012 he was barely one hundred seventy pounds. His cheeks were sunken, and that was made even worse when his teeth were lost—discarded most likely by someone calculating that he would never leave the hospital alive. Upon his return to the nursing home I could not pick him out in the day room—my own father!

At my request they returned him to soft-solid food—bananas and other soft fruit, oatmeal, vegetables cooked to mush—some things that required some chewing. And he put on a few pounds. We had no long-term hopes, but we didn't let on to that lack of optimism. I kept reading about treatments that were "in the pipeline," FDA approved trials, short-term miracles, and long-term horrors. If nothing else, we were cautious. For the time being, Dad was safe. His weight stabilized, he interacted with other residents. Occasionally, during a visit, he would pluck "son" out of his grab-bag of choices, more often I was his father, brother, cousin, and on one occasion, his minister. *That* was a visit.

More than once, more and more commonly in fact, I made the trip to see him and he was asleep. No amount of prodding would wake him. "Warren, Warren," the nurses would jiggle his shoulders. "Warren, Jack is here to see you, wake up." A few times his eyes opened, he smiled, but most times he just slept on. I would leave whatever laundered clothes I had for him, or replacement polos, sweat pants, sneakers, and drive home.

"Sorry," they said.

"It's a crap-shoot," I told them. "I understand."

"He was wide awake all morning, cooing."

I'll take your word for it.

"Why don't you call first?" they asked. I didn't bother to remind them that they had just said he was wide awake. . .never mind.

I left and rode past the house. I paid a neighborhood kid to cut the grass once a week. If it got overgrown, or needed weeding I made a note to call him: "the house is on the market, it has to look its best."

"No problem."

"Really?"

Sometimes I packed old clothes in case Dad was asleep, and I did yardwork myself, or vacuumed the house, cleaned counters or windows, painted baseboards, or simply made sure the house, the garage, the greenhouse were secure. I worried the homestead into spring. Rarely did I find realtor's calling cards. At first the agent said that winter months were awful for home sales, buyers made themselves scarce. "Wait until Spring." In Spring there was more work for us— trimming, edging, just trying to keep weeds at bay. I had the grass cut, but we struggled to keep the house in the shape the agent demanded. A yard service was out of the question and the budget despite the agent's constant carping. I simply went more often and the season's changed and I tried to keep up.

At some point I realized it was the real estate agent, not the house. Beyond the Multiple Listings publications, a single open house, she was doing nothing. There had not been a showing in weeks. When the contract renewal date arrived, we did not renew. A neighbor recommended a young go-getter at a different agency. I made the call. We met at the house. We shook hands and within a week we had three showings and an offer.

A week after that we had a contract and a lot less agita, and all a mere two weeks before the township warned us they would take the house for back taxes.

We exhaled and visited my father who was, by now, polite to us out of a lifetime habit of politeness. We kept up our weekly visits even though he had long ago forgotten that he even knew us, we were now even less familiar than someone he might have seen at Shop Rite years ago.

Late February 2014

The phone rang on a Wednesday morning as I was leaving for class. The caller I.D. told me it was Dr. Samuelson. I thought about ignoring it and letting it go to voice mail, but then I thought there might be a problem. I picked up.

"Jack?"

"Yeah."

"I, uhhh, wanted to keep you abreast of developments in the trial. I didn't want you think we were keeping things from you. We've had a minor setback."

"Phil Powers? We talked about this. He died of a heart attack."

"No, not Phil. Another patient."

"Died?"

"No, no. But he is slipping back, it seems. He still recalls a great deal, but his recall is not as sharp as it was a few weeks ago. Maybe it peaks and declines a little. Maybe it's nothing at all. We know so little at this point, it's impossible to say. But we haven't seen this before, and I thought you should know."

"Why?"

"Because I thought telling you was the right thing to do."

"I appreciate that. And the others? The fifty or so still clear?"

"It appears so. But this one has us on our toes."

"An anomaly?"

"God, I hope so. We are watching everyone very closely. I hate to say this, but we've seen this before. . ."

"So have I."

"Point taken. But success has never lasted this long. Before it was always bam, success—then sudden hive collapse syndrome, die-off. We're keeping our fingers crossed that this is not a repeat."

"Fingers crossed? Is that medical voodoo against your trial failing?"

"Fair enough."

"Nathan, my father will not be a lab monkey."

"No one's mother, or father is a lab animal. That is a terrible metaphor."

"Then make me a better one. So far, you've mentioned bees, monkeys, so by extension dogs, cats, rats, mice and any number of other animals they test on. Why not just say that sometimes animals just won't do? You need human subjects. Subjects! For Christ sake. Nathan, may I call you Nathan finally? Where are we, on a scale of one to ten, on human experiments? Let me ask you, if this were your father, how readily would you sign him up for your study, your trial, your experiment?

"Not a fair question. My father shows no signs of dementia."

"So what? It's a hypothetical. You're right you don't have to deal with this outside of your laboratory/nursing home. You're safe for now. But what if?"

"You don't know me, my life . . ."

"You're right. I don't. So, what's your point? We've been dancing this tango for years. Now there's 'a cure.' Sorry if I'm more than a little skeptical. I'm from Missouri, as they say. My father will not be a lab rat." Exhale.

That god-damned Samuelson-silence followed. Either he was going to hang up on me, or he was about to derail the whole conversation. Silence. Silence. More silence.

"Jack?"

"What?"

"This is just between us."

"I don't know what that means exactly, but okay."

"My grandmother,"

"Oh, Jesus, yeah."

"She's part of the study, the trial, the experiment."

"Why?"

"Because I believed what I was seeing."

"What about the new case, the guy slipping back? Are you second guessing yourself?

"It might be temporary, an anomaly. We'll have to see in a day, or a week if it was just a slip or a complete stumble back into the fog."

"Your grandmother?"

"She's just started. I don't expect to see any changes for a few days, maybe a week. The time is different for everyone."

"So, you waited."

"Of course."

"Of course, shit."

So, we delayed again. One day yes, the next day no. Then back to we'll think about it. All the while Dad drifted further away from us. Percentage wise Samuelson and his crew were beating the odds, I had to hand them that. Day after day, week after week their patients either popped back into the sunlight, so to speak, or stayed there far beyond any trial up to this point. Then, of course, someone's foot slipped— Nathan said a few quickly recovered their balance."

"Why? Why did they slip?"

"We don't know. A miscalculated dose, a hiccup in metabolism, or a temporary blood-chemical imbalance. We don't know. We're in new territory. 'There be dragons, or there be monsters,' isn't what you told me they wrote on old maps?"

"Not filling me with confidence."

"My own ebbs and flows. Some days I look out expecting to see the edge of the world and we're sailing straight toward it, the wind at our backs."

"A scary flat-earth metaphor, but it's honest."

"We're in flat-earth territory, Jack. Anti-amyloid drugs are the equivalent of Columbus on the Nina, Pinta and Santa Maria, blind faith, a theory and a prayer."

"And hope for the best."

"Well, we have a little more to go on than that. We no longer think there's just one cause, one disease, but a complex. We're combining the drug therapy with nutrition, environmental stimulation."

"Is this new, I don't recall hearing about this before?"

"It has been our collective approach all along. Until very recently we believed the primary mover was the drug, we hung our hat on the chemical component. Now we're not so sure. Tests are inconclusive, as they always are at this stage...But there is no arguing short-term observable results. Over fifty participants, sorry, patients, have returned to nearly one hundred percent clarity for months. At six months we will expand the study."

"Impressive."

"Thank you."

"I remember an earlier study was going gangbusters, then collapsed in a heap within a week."

"I've read about it too. I think you remember it right. But our study has already surpassed their longest success by two months."

"On a scale of one to ten how confident are you that this will work?"

"I've put my own grandmother in the trial, Jack."

This time it was my silence. "Mythology and history are littered with well-intentioned sacrifices," I muttered.

"Cut the academic bullshit, Jack. My grandmother, your father, this ain't theoretical. This is the real world, it's family. I have calculated the risk to save my mother's mother and I'm willing to go there. I can't offer you more than that."

"I agree, it's my cud to chew."

"Let me ask you a question. Have you looked at this from your father's point of view? Would he like to wake up clear-headed again, follow the plot of a movie or T.V. show, join in a conversation, or, like Phil Powers, grasp what his granddaughter had thought was lost forever? Sounds to me like you've only been thinking about this from your own perspective. Maybe he could, or would, accept the changes in his life and be happy to be back with you and Caitlin and Jon and whoever else might be left in his life. Sounds to me like you've just assumed he would pine away. You've always portrayed your father as a strong, pragmatic man. Okay, he would no doubt mourn your sister, your mother. We all mourn. He's, no doubt, had much to mourn in his life. After sadness most of us move on. Many experience joy again, find a way to celebrate still being alive. Imagine the stories he could tell about a long, happy life with your mother. What memories of Bonnie might he have that you know nothing about."

Nathan Samuelson stopped me in my tracks. I truly had not consciously attempted to change my point of view, to try out another one, such as how my father might have thought ten, twenty years ago.

I had watched him, watched his face—emotion chasing emotion—while we worked to cut free some limbs that had come down in a storm the night before (this was over thirty years ago). Rain sluiced down his face, my face, my sister's face. The storm had lessened in intensity in the morning, but it was still loud, brutal, inch-an-hour rain and huge claps of thunder. We were foolish to be working on a tree with all that lightening, but my father was afraid a big limb might come down on the house.

Around ten o'clock the loudest thunder clap I ever heard rattled the tree, the deck, the very house. Lightning struck a Locust across the street, there was a secondary explosion, and the tree caught fire. It was mayhem. We wrestled the biggest limbs into the yard and piled them roughly. The small stuff we left lying on the deck. We were communicating mostly with head shakes and hand signals. I was not even aware when my mother slid open the six-foot sliding glass door. "Warren," I saw my father turn and walk toward her. That's when his face went slack, then tightened. His eyes closed, not tired, but in resignation. I glanced at my sister. She shrugged.

We finished and went inside. My mother had towels ready. Caitlin and Jon, a little boy then, sat at the kitchen table. It was clear both Caitlin and my mother had been crying. Jon tinkered with a bowl of cereal.

Dad refused the towel and went straight upstairs. I waited until he was out of earshot. What happened?" I asked her. "Whatever you said to him out there shook him bad."

"Your grandfather died a few minutes ago."

"Jesus," Bonnie said, "we didn't know."

"How could you?" my mother said.

"Thank you, Dr. Samuelson," I said. "I had not thought from his perspective. That's selfish, isn't it?"

"I'd say you're being protective is all. He took care of you, now that he needs to be cared for you're just following his model. When the child becomes the parent, they rely on what they know, what they've learned, usually from that same parent. I'd say he taught you well."

"Listen, I have a class in an hour. Can we talk later? I do appreciate . . . I hope your grandmother is like . . .Phil Powers, without the heart attack, of course."

"I'll let you know."

"I think Caitlin and I need to get away this weekend, to talk, to think."

"Good idea."

"Maybe down to Chincoteague. Watch the ponies, the great blue herons."

"Call me when you get back."

I called Caitlin on my drive to school. "Pack our bags, okay. We're going to Chincoteague for the weekend. You're not working this weekend, are you?"

"It's only Wednesday."

"I know. Long weekend. And buy wine. Pinot, shiraz."

"Sounds serious."

"Sometimes somebody unexpected pries your brain open just enough to let the light in."

"Okay."

"And I could use some Neptune Spaghetti from AJ's."

"Let 'em go early, I'll be ready."

So, we escaped. We called Jon and asked him to please visit his grandfather. Caitlin had called ahead and made reservations at the Blue Heron Inn for four nights. She also called AJ's and made a Friday night reservation for two—just in case a fit of nice weather summoned the weekend warriors from D.C., Philly and points north and west.

So, we were covered. We could eat, sleep, drink and walk the wildlife loop if the weather cooperated. Personally, I couldn't have cared less about the weather, I had to wrap my head around what Samuelson had said to me. Damn him. I was beginning to grow comfortable with my rationalization that so much loss had created a world not worth returning to after years away.

Caitlin drove on the way down while I tried to reconstruct his argument, so I could lay it out for her and get her take on his reasoning. I first had to bush hog my old way of thinking—the underbrush and saplings of the argument that Bonnie's death, my mother's death just might destroy a mind and emotions made fragile in absentia. What if I were underestimating my father's resiliency, his ability to accept what had happened, to mourn, to suffer now what he had been unable to at the time of their deaths, and eventually embrace, like Phil Powers, what was left of his life. What if he was still the man who walked into the house, climbed the stairs and faced, alone, his own father's passing, did what he had to do in the privacy of his bedroom, then returned to us, calm, emotions in check, the man who called the funeral home, made arrangements, picked out a casket, oversaw the digging of the grave. The man who asked me if I would please say the eulogy for his father. Why would I expect someone else? How could I have ever anticipated a man who would collapse into grief and be unable to carry on when he had, more than once, dug the graves of relatives, his own grandparents, his brother's infant daughter.

Caitlin let me be, just drove with the radio barely audible in the background. The familiar landscape passed by without my seeing it. It was like riding and listening to a book on tape, the plot absorbing me, my own voice narrating. In a blink the three-hour trip was over.

"Best trip ever," I said.

"I doubt that," Caitlin told me. "I could see the whole story unfold on your face. Don't let anyone ever tell you you're a candidate for Rushmore. No sculptor could get your face to slow down long enough to capture a single pose."

"Sorry."

"For what?"

"For choosing to go through all of this stuff for the past, what, five, ten years?"

"I chose to ride out the storm, Jack. It was you who had no choice. Now, switch it off and think about a big bowl of Neptune Spaghetti and a salad with house artichoke vinaigrette. Oh, yeah, and a bottle of ice-cold Cavit Pinot Grigio."

"I can do that, Captain. And thank you."

"For what? You're paying for this weekend, mister."

I have always thought more clearly when I was walking. Thursday morning dawned clear and in the low fifties. We downed some motel-room coffee then drove to Mr. Baldy's for breakfast. After that we headed to Chincoteague's sister island, Assateague, once home to the famed Misty of Chincoteague, now to her ancestors. No private citizens live on the southern, Virginia end of the island. There is a visitor's center, some rangers-in-residence, but for most visitors the wildlife loop, a two-mile-long asphalt hiking/biking trail is the highlight. Coincidentally there are also a few miles of beautiful white sand beaches along the Atlantic. The loop skirts canals and marshes that fill and drain according to the season just as they fill and drain of birds during spring and fall migrations. Ducks, geese, swans, herons, cranes. You can carry thirty pounds of photographic equipment and see no birds whatsoever one day, go without any the next day and you may well find every bird on the Atlantic Flyway perching, swimming, wading and feeding in or along the tidal waters.

The islands were one of the first places Caitlin and I visited when we were dating. That is where we discovered each other on our long slow walks around the tidal pools, into the pine forest then newly ravaged by a beetle infestation, on side ventures to the ocean, then back, and around.

We were walkers, occasionally we biked, but we relished the slow pace of a walk, stopping to watch and name the birds, the white-tail and Sika deer, the famous ponies often found in groups of two or three, sometimes a dozen. Caitlin, a high-end amateur photographer, took some of her best pictures there. Eight by tens hang all over our house.

Even when the bird population was small between migrations there was always something to see, or at least look for: fox, snakes, once a small crowd of serious bird watchers with dangling binoculars hunched around a dung beetle. By 2014 the pine forest had recovered from the infestation in the eighties only to be hit again. Enough deciduous trees remained so the wooded sections of the loop were still green, but the ghosts of loblolly pines and red cedar haunted the edges and the depths of the forest.

"I doubt we'll live to see the pines bounce back again," Caitlin said. And we took three hours to make the one hour walk. Caitlin shot cranes and herons, tundra swans fighting like common street brawlers ("a woman to blame?"), and a four-foot-tall great blue heron who walked beside us for nearly a quarter of a mile beside a tidal pool where we also watched muskrat swimming. Above us a murmuration of starlings did their best balletic moves over the water for a full five minutes.

Back in our room we drank some wine and decided on Edda's for dinner on Saturday. My mind was, for the moment, a blissful tableau rasa. I was ready to talk—maybe on Friday. Caitlin seemed content to let me vegetate. Birds, ponies, pictures, deer, black squirrels, pictures. Repeat.

Thursday evening, we went to Don's for shrimp and the salad bar. Upstairs later we listened to local music in Chatty's lounge, then drove back to our temporary home. I fell asleep watching Rachel Maddow.

The last thing I thought about was Neptune spaghetti, salad with artichoke dressing, and ice-cold Pinot Grigio at AJ's Friday night.

And AJ's didn't disappoint. We sat near a window, so we could watch the creek. We reminisced about the time we sat on the patio in the dark and watched a rocket launch from Wallop's Island—a noise as loud as the thunder on the day my grandfather died, a brilliant light that slowly rose into the black sky. It was one of those moments.

From behind her menu Caitlin said, "So what did the good doctor say to you that has you so, what, contemplative? Rattled? Withdrawn?"

So, for the next fifteen minutes—with time out to order—I laid out the conversation as best I could remember it. And Caitlin listened without interrupting me. "So maybe he's right, maybe my thinking has been clouded, or just plain wrong," I concluded.

My wife laid her wine glass on the table and stared at me. "A compelling argument from the young doctor. Logical. Reasonable. But how many patients have we gone to see who have a situation like ours, like Dad's? None. Phil and Nancy were wonderful, but Phil's story was nothing like your father's. The world he reentered was, for all intents and purposes, unchanged. No adaptation or acceptance required."

"True enough. But what about the argument that Dad has weathered countless losses, so why wouldn't, or couldn't he do it again?"

"How old was your father in 1987?"

"Sixty, umm, five. Why?"

"That's why."

"That's why what?"

"That was twenty-seven years ago. He's not sixty-five, he's ninety-two, and in poor health."

"But what if Samuelson is right?"

"What if he's not? What if your gut is right, Jack? Think about the sorrow. We had a little bit of time to recover from Bonnie's death before your mother died. He'd be hit with both losses at the same instant. Try to imagine that."

I drained my glass of Cavit. "Really? This is supposed to help me? Guide me?"

"Yes. Now eat your spaghetti."

On Sunday we packed and left. We had always wanted to live on the island, but there were no opportunities for an academic and a nurse. We came as often as possible, but we couldn't swing a full time move. Crossing the causeway going north and west was always sad.

We stopped at Tall Pines before driving the rest of the way home. Jon, the nurse told us, had just left. He had come every day since Thursday. "Only once was your father asleep, but he stayed for an hour anyway."

He was sitting at a table by himself, his bib still on from lunch. I took it off of him and threw it in the trash can. "We need to get you some new sneakers," I told him, "these are worn down and not befitting a man of your station." He nodded. He only left the wheelchair now to be put to bed, so the sneakers were more worn out than worn down. Caitlin did not smile at my attempted levity."

I told him we had been on Chincoteague for a long weekend. I told him about the birds and the other animals we had seen, the meals we had eaten. It was a familiar place to him, he and my mother had gone there for decades, he knew the place better, perhaps, than Caitlin and I did. I sometimes wondered if he returned to the island when he traveled through time looking for some comforting time to settle back into. I wondered if he walked the loop (he was a big-time walker too), ate clams, oysters, flounder and drum at Don's or Bill's or Edda's. I wondered where he went, what he did now in his mind that he had done then, to whom he told his stories. I wondered what had interested or excited him enough long ago to return to now. I hope it was all vivid— Phil told us his memories were cinematic and in technicolor and Dolby sound.

Just as leaving Chincoteague that morning had made me sad, leaving him made me sadder. I have read a great deal about Alzheimer's disease, the suspected causes, the possible treatments, the effects on victims and the devastating effects on helpless loved ones, especially the care givers. Most catastrophic diseases ultimately destroy one person, Alzheimer's and Parkinson's wipe out whole families.

There was, is, a growing literature by and about the people who sacrifice their lives—husbands, wives, daughters, sons, sometimes nieces and nephews. Some take years to recover after their loved one dies, some never do. It is a literature of true heroism, and a literature of exhaustion and devastation. Care is often performed anonymously, the patient doesn't know, and the world rarely hears about what caregivers do thanklessly, and sometimes while impoverishing themselves. Yet who do you get angry with, and where do you vent that anger?

Except for my mother and the long, slow toll it exacted on her and her health, we were a lucky family. Dad was cared for, he was safe, we could go to bed at night and sleep knowing that good people three shifts a day were doing their best for him. Yeah, having to leave him there was sadder than leaving any mere island.

I waited for a week after we got home from our long weekend to call Dr. Samuelson. I still had no answer for him about enrolling my father in his study, trial, experiment, whatever. Once upon a time—a week ago—I thought I was certain where I stood on the matter, then I talked to Nathan, and his argument shook me good. I wavered. Then I talked to Caitlin and I was right back where I started, and once again not so firm as to want to pull the plug on the whole idea.

I called my son from my office. He was at work and couldn't talk, but he did promise to call me back at home in the evening. Goody, more time to stew. I decided to back off on thinking about it for a while. I graded some essays. I gave up after two, I decided it was unfair to take out my frustration on their twenty-year-old brand of illogic which seemed in the moment as leaky as my own.

I cleaned my desk instead.

I had an office-mate once—another school, another lifetime—who kept a stack of paper on his desk. It leaned, it teetered and threatened to topple and crush whoever had the misfortune of being in its path. To anyone other than him it appeared to be years' worth of old tests, essays, memos, letters and academic junk mail randomly piled, sheet on sheet, year after year. But I happened to be at my desk one day when a graduating senior stopped by and asked for a paper he had written when he was a freshman. He was assembling a portfolio and remembered he had received an A from a notoriously tough grader. Without hesitation, Tom reached into the exact geological layer of petrified wood and extracted the very paper requested.

I was stunned.

When the student left our office, I said, "that was a remarkable stunt. How did you do that?"

"Luck," he laughed.

"Bullshit," I said. "I've seen you do that before. Do you have eidetic memory or something?"

"No, nothing like that."

"So, serendipitously you cram your meat hook into a three plus foot stack of paper and pull out, by luck, the exact piece of paper requested. No , unh uh."

He laughed. "I have a general idea where the top of the pile was at any given year. Remember, I've been in this office for many years— long before you got here, and I'll be here long after you've moved on. So, I have a general idea about how fast my mountain rises," he said, jerking his thumb toward the stack.

"So how fast does the stack grow?"

"Six or eight inches a year."

"And it's only that tall after all your years here?"

"Oh, no. About ten years ago the V.P. came to see me about something or other. She took one look at the office and hightailed it back to the admin building and wrote a memo threatening my employment if I didn't clean up Mount Misery—her name, not mine— so I had maintenance come with their rolling garbage cans and take it down on a weekend." He shook his head.

"And on Monday you started rebuilding."

"Precisely, Dr. Wilson. Very astute of you."

By the time my desktop was once again visible, my office hours were over. I packed my papers in my briefcase and locked the door— not a single step closer to a decision, but happy I had not unnecessarily lambasted a dozen or more ill-conceived masterpieces.

Jon called me back around seven o'clock. I had just taken a hot dog off the grill. I put it back on and shut off the gas and hoped it wouldn't dry out."

"What's up?"

"You called me."

"Oh, yeah. I wanted to thank you for going to see your grandfather, the nurse told us you stayed an hour while Grandpa slept."

"You don't have to thank me."

"Okay. Do you have a few minutes?"

" Yup, what's on your mind?"

"The study."

"No surprise there. I thought you and Mom were going to hash it out on Chincoteague."

"We did. Sort of. Look…last week I thought I had my mind made up. I thought there were too many risks, that the risks from learning that a daughter and a wife were dead, the homestead sold, over half a century of collections sold off or sent to the junk yard might be too much for a person to absorb in a single swallow."

"No argument from me. I can't even imagine what a blow that would be. I know Grandpa is strong, but who knows what's happened to his mind in the past four years."

"Then I had a talk with Dr. Samuelson."

"Sure. And he said?"

For the next ten minutes I tried to recreate our conversation the same way I'd done for Caitlin. Jon listened as I recounted his points.

"A reasonable enough argument."

"That's what your mother said too."

"Okay. And?"

"And then she made mince-meat out of his logic. Said what if he's wrong, what if your grandfather isn't the same stolid guy able to rebound from emotional shock like he used to."

147

"Who knows what happens in the fog, as you call it. There could be profound changes that have already happened in his brain. Mom has a point."

"And that's exactly my problem. I thought I had made up my mind, I thought I was ready to lay out my rationale to you and your mother. Then Samuelson made me question myself. So, then I talked to your mother and now I'm right back where I started, but now I have a lingering doubt nibbling on my resolve."

"When in doubt, talk it out."

"Where have I heard that before? I thought that's what we were doing."

"We are, but Mom and I are emotionally invested. We can't make an objective decision any more than you can."

"But in the end, it has to be you who signs on the dotted line, Dad. What you decide, we'll abide by. Simple as that. But what about a third party, someone who has no skin in the game?"

"Like?"

"Colleagues? Friends?"

"No one's business but ours."

"I get that, but what about a fresh perspective? Talk to someone who hasn't been dealing with this for years like we have. Who knows, maybe we're missing something. Maybe there's something really obvious staring at us and we just don't see it. Do you know anyone in the Psychology Department you could talk to?"

"I only know them from faculty meetings. No one I'd want to engage with about my father's life and future."

"I have to tell you, I'm really afraid we're running out of time. Over the weekend, while Grandpa was sleeping, I started to think back over the past few years, and it seems the distances between landmarks on his timeline are growing shorter and shorter. Has Dr. Samuelson suggested that there might be a statute of limitations on this treatment?"

"None that he's mentioned. He told me he's enrolled his own grandmother in the study. I gather she's about Grandpa's age."

"That's interesting, I didn't know about that."

"He only told me last Wednesday when he was making his latest pitch."

"What's her story?"

"I don't know, he didn't volunteer very much."

March 2014

Caitlin has had, since she was a little girl, insights, premonitions—she sees what's coming before it's even on the horizon. Her mother even took her to be tested in New York. She was encouraged by the testers to trust her instincts, to accept what she saw happening before it happened. She had dreams, day time and night time dreams where she saw what would happen the next day, or the next, or the next week. It was scary how what she saw actually happened, she told me, not always, at least not where she could verify it—but a high percentage of the time she predicted when her patients would die, and most times she was right by a day or two. "There are patterns," she told me, "people plot and plan, they wait for family members or friends to come, or go. And then they die. It's not always as random as you think, as arbitrary. People often times call their own shots."

"'Splain yourself, Lucy."

"Okay, look, I had a patient, young, mid-thirties, he made his brother promise he would be with him at the end—he predicted he would die before his thirty fifth birthday. Yeah, yeah, the brother agreed. At thirty-four and a half he goes into heart failure. The brother sits with him for hours. He's in a drug-induced coma. Around six-seven in the morning the brother, who'd talked to his younger brother all night, tells him he's going home to shower, get some breakfast and he'll be back. His vitals were good. He was out, but he was hanging in."

"So, the brother leaves…"

"So, the brother leaves, drives home, showers and the phone rings. It's the hospital. His brother chose that tiny window of time to die."

"Coincidence?" I asked her, "heart attack?"

"Coincidence, maybe, but no heart attack. But I've seen it a hundred times. My friends have too. You doubt it, that's okay."

"Are you seeing my father's death?"

"I think so."

"I know he's ready. There's no one to wait for, except for us they're all gone. And we've all been to see him many times. He's just waiting."

"Waiting for you to give him permission to die."

"Or to bring him back. He's strong enough to stay, I think. He could be with us for a few more years. He'd love to say he outlived his father by a year or two. It was always competition with them. Who had the first tomato ripen. Who had the last pepper in the fall. If you saw something you were certain of, you'd tell me, right, Caitlin?

"Yeah, if I were sure."

"Promise?"

"Jack."

*

"Jack, he's *your* father. I've told you what I think, Jon's told you what he thinks, and Nathan's chipped in his two cent's worth. I hate to say this, my love, but it's up to you, and we're behind you one hundred percent whatever that decision is. I see you drive down to see your father, and whether he's asleep or awake I see you come home and you're ten year's older. The choice is finally yours, not ours. I would love to take the weight off of you. But I can't. I'm sorry."

The day after my talk with Jon, I hid out in my office. Since it was not a teaching day and I had no appointments scheduled, no one really knew I was on campus. I closed my door, I sat at my desk, I disappeared into my head. I replayed dozens of scenes with my father going back to my first memory of the squirrel in the park. I tried to imagine him watching the Hindenburg pass over Chapel Hill, New Jersey, May 6, 1937, on its way to its destruction in Lakehurst a few hours later when he was fifteen years old. He had talked very little about seeing the Morro Castle burn off of Asbury Park in 1934 or watching one of the Twin Lights in Highlands extinguished so the Germans could not identify the only two-tower lighthouse on the east coast. I thought about the two floaters (one of them a German soldier) he found off of Sandy Hook as a young private in the Army months

151

prior to shipping out to the west coast and finally to the Southwest Pacific, the Philippines.

I had, of course, only his stories to go on and a few brief entries on some blank pages of a survival G.I. handbook titled "Tagalog." I did not try to grade papers on my paper-grading day. I sat instead and remembered the stories I overheard when I was very young, a few quips in the barber shop, censored stories leaked when I was older. They were a patchwork, a gallimaufry, a miscellany, a hodge-podge, a mélange, a jumble, a salmagundi—they were the puzzle I had been trying to assemble all of my life, and damnit, pieces were missing—not many, but pieces were missing, and the image was skewed. I wanted to know it complete, and I wondered if, out of the fog, my father would make it so.

I didn't think my father had tried to mislead or lie, I think he did not want to face again what he had already confronted once. He wanted to put into time-appropriate boxes those events, those images, those emotions. A small amount of those emotions had spilled out over time, I spent the hours trying to stitch what I knew for certain into a wampum belt—a walum olum—of his history. But it refused to cohere, too many pieces were missing—withheld or misplaced, so I finally gave up. It was not my job or my right to intrude. I knew what I knew, and I had to be content with that.

I tried to imagine my son probing the corners of my life. Not much to hide, but I didn't like the idea of snooping, prying, going where I had no business going. So, I quit. I assembled what I knew and quit for the day, I went home, poured a Pinot and planned the next visit to Tall Pines.

I wanted a chance to talk to my father, man to man, to explain why I decided what I decided, to get his approval—somehow, someway—to maybe catch a glimmer of acceptance, the barest nod, an unintended, but unmistakable wink.

I remembered the look on Phil's face when he told us about his granddaughter, and I tried to imagine Jon reuniting with his grandfather.

That was Tuesday. I was going to Tall Pines on Thursday. I was going without announcement or ceremony—I always showed up unannounced just to see the daily round, the routine, how my father was dressed, shaved, bathed, fed. He was always a model—spit shined and spic and span.

One place I rarely went was my father's room. It was Spartan. He had a bed, a dresser, a closet and a decoupaged photo of he and my mother when they were engaged, given to them years before by my sister. It hung above his bed. Every nurse, every aid who came to the room commented on what a gorgeous couple they had been. But it depressed me. I had glimpsed rooms that were resplendent with plush chairs, tables, vases, artwork—all of which simply got in the way of daily care. The fluff and bother of those rooms was, I understood, to assuage the guilt of relatives who never visited. Plush was not what my father needed. I cringed when I saw the bare-bones of his existence, but he only slept in the room, the rest of his time was spent in a day room surrounded by music I hoped he remembered, people he could at least enjoy, and food that kept him alive.

If the Wilsons were wealthy people, it might have been different, but life had settled into a practical round of bathing, eating, recreation and sleeping. And I hated what it had become. Every visit, it seemed, my father slipped further away from us. At first it was memory, then it was speech, now it was mobility. One by one his dignities were taken away and a man who had depended on no one since he was eighteen years old now depended on strangers for everything. He had made me promise not to let him wind up in this place or one like it, and I had failed him. Now he depended on an absolute stranger to change his diaper. He would be mortified, I thought, so I had to be mortified for him. He didn't know.

Thank god, he didn't know.

When I arrived at the Juniper unit, I spoke to the nurse at the desk. "Mr. Wilson, how are you?"

"I'm well, thank you. I want to have a private conversation with my father today."

"Oh, okay. There's a private room off of the common area. I think it's free. I can check if you want me to. Or you could talk with your father in his room." She must have read my face. "Umm, if it is free you can use it as long as you like…You do understand that he probably won't understand what you want to talk to him about, right?"

"Yeah, I get that. I just need some father and son time. Not the day room, not the activities and music."

The room was free.

"I can have an aid bring him to the room for you."

"Thank you, I can do that, it's no problem."

"Whatever you like."

I shrugged. "I like to do what I can for him. It's little enough these days."

"Mr. Wilson, some of these people haven't had a visitor in years."

I wheeled him into the room, closed the door, and we faced each other. "Dad," he raised his eyebrows and stared straight at me. Dad, what you have, Alzheimer's disease, okay, they think they have a cure." The lights were out in his eyes.

Jesus.

"Dad, I want to tell you, even if you don't understand. I know you talked to me when I was a baby. I know you must have coo'd and burbled and gushed over me, first born and you a new father. I know you did. What secrets you must have told me. I want Jon to know those stories too. 'Best damn Yankee story teller,' my old grad school roommate called you. And you were."

"Coo," he said.

*

I dialed Nathan Samuelson's office. It rang and rang. I wondered if they had caller I.D. and had been instructed not to answer my calls. *Screw him. I don't need to talk to him. I can find...*" Hello, Dr. Samuelson's office, can you hold?" *Please hold. Will you hold?* I held.

"Thank you for holding. How may I help you?"

"This is Jack Wilson, I'd like to make an appointment with the doctor."

"May I ask what this is in reference to?"

"You may not. He'll know."

"Oh. Let me see what's available."

"A Tuesday or Thursday, please."

"Okay." Pause. "I have a 11 o'clock next Tuesday, or 3 o'clock next Thursday."

"Eleven on Tuesday," I said.

"Would you like a reminder call on Monday?"

"Not necessary, thank you."

"Then we'll see you next Tuesday at 11."

"Thank you."

*

I cancelled the rest of my Friday classes and went home. No broken hearts over that, I was sure. I dropped my jacket and briefcase in the hall and went straight to my study.

Rilke's "Sonnets to Orpheus" had always given me great comfort. I don't know why, I never really tried to figure it out. When I opened the Poulin translation and began to read, I disappeared from whatever was bothering me—

Dance the Orange

Wait…that taste… it's already flown.

…Just a little music, a stamping, a drone:

You warm maidens, you silent maidens,

Dance the taste of fruit we experience!

Dance the orange. Who can forget it?

How. Drowning in itself, it struggles to

Deny its sweetness. You possess it.

It preciously converts itself to you.

Dance the orange. The warmer season.

Weave around you, so it ripely shines

In the air of its homeland! Radiant, reveal

Fragrance after fragrance! Create the liaison

Between the pure, forbidding rind,

And the juice, with which this happy fruit is filled!

Whatever made me cry the first time I read this poem as young man on a cold wet day when I couldn't go to work, worked its magic all over again. My gut knew exactly what the poem meant—and my brain had a small idea.

*

On Saturday morning the phone rang. "It's Samuelson," Caitlin said, glancing at the screen.

I picked up. "Hello."

"I see you made an appointment for Tuesday."

"I did. How's your grandmother?"

"Glimmers," he said. "Yesterday she recognized me. When she calls me by my nick name, I'll celebrate."

"Maybe today."

"Maybe so."

"Why are you in the office on Saturday?"

"Saturday's special? What do you want to see me about on Tuesday?"

"It'll wait."

"Phase two of the study is going to close next week."

"Will there be a phase three?"

"I don't know. Maybe. So far no one else has regressed. So maybe, the bigger the study…you know."

"Let me ask you, what if someone doesn't respond to the drug, what if someone gets worse?"

"It's never happened, Jack. Not once. Some patients, as I told you, slip backwards over time, but everyone improves for a while."

"What percentage 'slip backwards?'"

"Maybe five percent."

"What other statistics have you gathered?"

"Jesus Christ, Jack. I've already told you I can't offer a guarantee. If our history tells us anything, it tells us we can bring your father back for weeks, months, maybe longer. The study isn't old enough to predict beyond that. I know your concerns, I know what your family has faced in a short period of time. It's probably unique within the study group. I can't tell you how any patient will respond when they regain memory, speech, any ability they've lost. I agree with you, okay? I always have. Abundance of caution. I'm not pitching or selling what I have to offer you, you have the whole package. I've laid out what we've done— successes, failures. Everything is on display."

"I appreciate that, I do. We do"

"We'll talk on Tuesday."

I slumped back into my chair. *How different.* My mother's decline had been sudden, not completely unexpected, but sudden. The call came during class— "I think you need to come, now." Two hours later I was there, my mother was still conscious, but barely coherent.

"I think," the nurse said while standing next to the bed, "that this is…"

I shot her a look that shut her up. I motioned for her to follow me to the hallway. "You know my mother can hear you even though she's semi-conscious, right?"

"Probably."

"Then why would you say she was going to die?"

"She is."

"What part of this did they not cover in nursing school? Even people in a coma can hear. Why would you scare them with talk of their dying?"

"I'm sorry, I didn't think…"

"Exactly. You know her, you know she's scared to death to die and you talk about her dying like she wasn't there. Christ."

*

After I talked with Samuelson, I felt untethered, unanchored, ungrounded. I looked at Caitlin, "let's go to the Poconos."

"The Poconos? Really? We don't go to the Poconos. We've never been to the Poconos."

"I was there. As a kid. Nearly drowned. In a pool at a motel."

"Where is this coming from?"

"I don't know."

"Go for a walk. You think better when you walk."

"Wanna go?"

"You need to walk by yourself."

I keep four walking sticks hanging in the back hall, another in my study, and one that screws together in three pieces in the trunk of my car. I grabbed one in the hall, a sad, timeless face of an old, bearded man carved into the grip, vines twisting down toward the ground. I leaned the stick against the passenger seat then got in and drove to the piece of the Appalachian Trail that runs through our town about two miles from our house.

It's an unremarkable stretch of the trail, but affords day hikers a path, some lovely scenery, and for some, a respite from quotidian concerns and complications. Through hikers, if they remember it at all, recall only a fleeting question: this is New Jersey?"

My stick and I took a walk. I glanced at my watch, it was one thirteen. On the trail I walk at about a two and half mile per hour pace. I gave myself an hour out and an hour back—five miles and plenty of sunlight still left in the day.

William Wordsworth liked to compose his poems while walking in the Lake District around Dove cottage, his stride maintaining an iambic meter. No Wordsworth, but I quickly fell into a rhythm that quieted my mind. One foot in front of the other over level ground gave me a feeling of safety where I could gather and organize my thoughts in a way I could not at home or in the office.

It felt good to surrender to the purely mechanical task of walking, propelling my body forward on three legs. My walking stick provided an accent to the left/right beat of my feet moving up the trail. It was cold, but I soon felt a warmth. And then a sweat under my coat. If I kept moving, it would not turn to a chill.

Thoughts walking. Where had I heard or read that?

I have two thoughts, like two legs, both mine but on opposite sides: bring Dad back and trust that the old strength when facing loss will still be part of who he is. OR leave him be in his final years, oblivious and beyond the hurt and ensuing sadness that might very well kill him before his time. Left/right-tap. Left/right-tap. Back and forth. I set my stick down lightly along with my right foot—not there for support or balance, but there should I stumble, should one foot or the other catch on a small rock and twist or slide.

At two fifteen I stopped, a little winded, a little sweaty, and a lot relieved. I had always been a walker—as a boy I walked to my grandparents' house on Chapel Hill, then home, maybe four miles round trip. At age twelve I walked to my other grandparents' house, about seven miles—then someone drove me home.

I sat on a rock. My body felt like it was still in motion—one, two, left, right, and then the accent of the stick striking dirt, or duff along with my right foot. I rested for just a few minutes then headed back toward the car—two and a half miles away—and beyond that, home. I had secretly hoped the rhythm would magically deliver an insight, an answer that had been locked inside that walking iamb since the time of Wordsworth. It didn't. I felt calmer, but still conflicted.

March 18, 2014

7am

I got up and showered.

7:15

Caitlin was in the kitchen drinking coffee. We made small talk, my wife of a third of a century and I. I buttered an asiago bagel, then only nibbled around the edges. Outside it was one of those March mornings where fog seemed to drip from the trees; traffic, especially the school buses, crawled, and it was quiet, sans birdsong.

"So, what are you going to tell Samuelson today?" She double-handed her coffee mug like someone in an old Maxwell House commercial.

"I honest to god wish I knew."

"Really? Any leanings?"

"Depends on what minute you're referring to."

"That undecided?"

"Yup."

"So, the walk didn't help."

"The walk was a balm, not a cure. I hoped the rhythm would trigger something—anything. It didn't. I am going to be as surprised as Samuelson and you and Jon by what comes out of my mouth today. Save my father or leave him be. Caitlin, I honestly don't know the right answer, I see moats and pitfalls in both answers. I don't even know if there is a *right* answer." Click.

8 am

I brewed a second cup of coffee and settled into my lounge chair. I rarely did this before 8 pm. The day was not designed to be but was shaping up to be out of the ordinary—I decided to let it find its shape, its boundaries and trajectory.

"Two roads diverged in a yellow wood." Yeah, that's obvious. "And I took the road less travelled by." Great. Which one would that be? Thanks, person talking in my head.

I clicked on "Morning Joe" and tried to silence whoever or whatever was trying to engage me. I couldn't get comfortable. I fidgeted and twisted. I finally gave up and walked fifteen minutes on the treadmill. *I'll calm you one way or the other, damn you.*

8:20

I made a pepper and egg sandwich and slid it onto a hard roll. I sat and watched Joe and Mika. The entire conversation flowed like water under a bridge. What? Who are they talking to? *Whoa, this going to require you to be present. Got it? Slow down.*

Relaxation exercise. Ten minutes. I quieted everything from the top of my head to my hammer toes and up the other side. While relaxed, I tried some guided imagery, and returned to the meadow. I exhaled, out far and in deep.

I flew. Relaxed. I often flew over the meadow and saw the little pond, the trees. I found a stream and glided above it, swooping between branches, diving, rising, weightless, happy. For ten more minutes I soared, that's about as long as I could fly I had found out years ago. Then I could no longer stay aloft, I could not follow the stream's meander. I slammed back into my body, relaxed state or not.

I could no longer fly or trick myself into flight. As quickly as I launched, I tumbled to a landing. Session over and none the worse for wear.

8:43

My head was calm, bordering on numb. I was content to continue in that state five minutes more. Peaceful, I would have stayed there forever if I could, but I too quickly returned to the realization that I had to shake it off, get with the program, as we used to say. But the calm, sober state felt so good. I wanted to linger, maybe return to the state of deep relaxation. But no, the silent alarm goes off—*time to move on. You have an appointment to keep in a little less than two hours.*

9:02

I lingered in the closet picking out slacks, a shirt and shoes. I absently wondered what I should be wearing when my father saw me again for the first time in four years. What would he most remember? I stopped. *This is absurd. What the hell would Dad care what you were wearing?* I was jumpy and nauseous. Even if the drugs worked, and there was a very small chance that they wouldn't, the effects would be days, maybe weeks away. *The only one seeing your sartorial splendor will be Nathan Samuelson, Twit.*

I pulled down a pair of jeans, a blue broadcloth button down, a pair of Clarks slip-ons and a khaki corduroy jacket. Teaching attire.

My phone vibrated on the dresser. "Hey, Dad. Just wanted to tell you, whatever you decide…"

"Thanks, Jon. I almost think I know, but I'm going to keep an open mind. Listen, why don't you join us for dinner at Panzerotti's"?

"Sorry, got a date tonight."

"Bring Alexis, she ain't no stranger ya know."

"We could do that, then head out afterwards."

"While the old folks head home for a head start on half-a-day of sleep."

"Funny. We'll meet you, at what, five? Six?"

"Say six, ish."

"See you then. Thanks."

"Later."

In the kitchen Caitlin hugged me. "Ooooh, you smell good."

"Thanks, it's an homage. Old Spice. The few times I went to church with my father he wore a gray suit, black brogans and Old Spice. That's what church smells like to me."

"Good for you. Always smelled like dead flowers left over from weddings and funerals to me."

"Nice."

"Not really." Silence. "Jack, are you all right? Do you want me to go with you? You look like you're aging right in front of my eyes."

"I'm okay. No. And I am. Add to that I invited Jon and Alexis to have dinner with us tonight at Panzerotti's, six-ish."

"Oh, good. We haven't seen her since New Year's Eve. Seems like a life time ago, huh?"

9:20

When I was twelve or thirteen, I went away to Boy Scout camp for the first time. By day two I was so homesick they had to call my parents to come and fetch me. I wept. I sobbed. I risked being mocked unmercifully. They, a camp functionary, took me to a cabin where a very calm older man sat among chunks and slabs of wood. He spoke very little, and he took his time to choose a piece of pine from his pile.

"What do you see in this piece of wood?" he asked me.

"Nothing," I sobbed.

"Let me show you what's there," he said, "will you stop crying so I may show you what I see in this piece of pine? Your parents are coming tomorrow."

"Yes," I said, calming, rescue on the way. It was late at night. The rest of my troop were long asleep, not at all homesick, some very glad to be away."

"Here," he said in the deepest, most peaceful voice I had ever heard. The piece of wood was maybe a foot long and one-inch square. He took a folding knife out of his pocket and pulled out the blade. In a few deft strokes he narrowed the block of wood to a blade, leaving a large chunk on one end.

With a simple pen knife, he whittled a blade. I had seen someone whittle before, my grandfather had carved a few dolls for Bonnie. I had a small sling-shot he carved for me in my dresser drawer, and I had a tiny whittled face I carried in my pocket for good luck.

Chips and shavings flew from his tiny knife blade. First a face began to emerge, then a tall head dress, feathers, a nose, a mouth and

163

eyes appeared as magically as the images in my father's dark room, but these were three dimensional—within minutes the head of a Lenni Lenape chief sat on the long blade of a letter opener. Regal. Royal. Magical.

I had long ago stopped crying and watched his knife slice away everything that did not comprise the chief's face. I was mesmerized. I no longer wanted my parents to come and take me home. The same mysteries happened there, at the camp, in a small cabin—a picture blooming out of developer. I felt at home, somehow.

I stayed the week. I went to see the carver—Morley—every day. They had not really called my parents to come and get me. They knew this calm, carving shaman had charmed a generation of homesick boys with his skills.

I suddenly knew I wanted to become a carver, to transform blocks of wood into real shapes in the world, to make something shapely and beautiful out of almost nothing. The knife failed me, but I found my blocks of wood in the classroom. C'est la vie.

Like my guided imagery, my reverie ended with a jolt. Now I was running late. Shit.

I gave the letter opener to my parents when they picked me up at the end of the week. No one, not my scout master, not the Director of the camp, not Morley breathed a word of my meltdown. As I put on my pants and shirt and jacket I calculated how many years ago that had been—over fifty years—and I wondered when Morley had died, where, and how. Ghoulish, maybe, but he had given me something very precious, a way of seeing, of knowing the world the way he must have known it, how to see the Indian chief in a simple block of pine wood. I said as much of a prayer for him as I was capable of.

Why am I remembering fifty plus year old experiences? Simple. Remembering what is more appealing than what I have to do today that is fixed in time. Screw up today, and you can't do it over. I looked at my finished self in the mirror. Enhh. Presentable. This is what my students saw. Okay.

I pegged my decision on a two hour's drive to Tall Pines, what I could not decide in the past months, three months, I would magically decide as I drove south to the county of my birth. Somewhere along the way the answer hung like the gold ring on the carousel at Asbury Park. I had only to ride the magic jackass on the outer perimeter, lean out far enough, hook my pointer finger into the ever refilling ring dispenser and be lucky enough to round the circle at just the moment when the gold ring emerged—correct answer, problem solved, the rest of my life a congratulatory, back-slapping, what-a-good-boy-am-I party. Right!

Gotta go.

I heard not a word of what Caitlin said to me. I started my car, aimed it south, and for the next two hours I could not say what I saw, heard, smelled, tasted or thought. I simply drove.

I pulled into the parking lot at Tall Pines and parked my car. Samuelson could wait. I needed to gather my thoughts.

And what I thought about is how a life could come down to a few minutes in a parking lot held in someone else's hands—my hands. I thought about, "If I'm not living, just existing, let me go." I thought about hearing the old stories in the old familiar voice again, how much Jon would love to hear the stories he had never heard or had forgotten.

11:02

I got out of the car and walked toward the entrance.

"Dr. Wilson."

"Hello."

"Dr. Samuelson is just finishing his rounds. He'll be with you in a second. Coffee?"

"No thank you."

11:05

"Jack."

"Nathan. How's your grandmother?"

"Well, this morning she called me Nate."

"A good sign?"

"My nick name. The sign I was waiting for."

"Good for you."

"Thanks. We have now successfully returned fifty-three people, brought them out of the fog. They are enjoying their families, Jack."

"How many have had to face major changes?"

He sighed. "Most have only been gone a short time, a few months, a couple of years at most, I think. Their families are intact."

12:15

After my meeting with Samuelson, I just drove around. The decision no longer hung heavily over me, but now the consequences of my decision took its place. I drove past the house, stopped and talked to neighbors and gave them an update on Dad's condition. I said nothing to them about what I had decided, I never even mentioned the study at all. I didn't feel comfortable talking about it even though I had known these people nearly my whole life. It would be enough telling Caitlin and Jon.

The new owners of my parents' house had not kept up the gardens, they were weedy, and some had simply been abandoned, cut down with a lawnmower. The trees looked hacked rather than pruned, the house merely occupied, not lived in. I felt sorry and sad I had made the effort. Except for the neighbors I got to see, the whole venture made me sick.

I rode around town, my true home town—past my elementary school, the library, the fire house with the baseball field behind it. I parked my car and walked the bases, stood on the pitcher's mound, the scene of my earliest victories and defeats. I walked up the red clay hill and looked down into the gulley that had once held trolley tracks that had been a distant memory even in the fifties. I drove down every familiar and unfamiliar street and avenue in town. I drove to the supermarket/liquor store strip mall that had been the Lewis farm when I was a boy. I drove to the store that had also housed the Post Office long ago, to the church that was not my church but one I attended occasionally when I was thirteen and fourteen to meet girls at youth group meetings. I drove to the largest yacht harbor on the east coast, then to the highest geographical point on the coast—Maine to Florida. I sat in my car for an hour and looked across a river, a bay and an ocean at lower Manhattan.

When I had exhausted water, ball fields and strip malls, I drove to the cemetery to visit my mother's and sister's graves. I talked to them. They were the first to know what I had decided. I could only imagine their agreement or disappointment. Had I pleased or displeased them? I placed pebbles on their foot stones, as my mother had taught me to do. Calling cards, she called them.

I left my car by the family plot and walked back to the divot that had been Wilson's pond, a mere indentation in the earth filled now with mature maples and white birch, conifer saplings and grasses. *In fifty years, no one would suspect there had ever been a pond there.* The banks had already eroded, and it looked like just a low spot in the woods, just one more unremarkable feature left over, perhaps, by a long-ago glacier.

I said goodbye to my dead and drove away. I stopped and ate two slices of pizza—it was so much better here than where I lived in the mountains. It was one of the things I missed most, that and the sub sandwiches. What I did not miss was the traffic, the shoulder to shoulder people everywhere, the prime reason we had moved decades before.

At some point between leaving Samuelson and pointing my car north, I began to doubt the decision I had finally made. I thought about driving back to Tall Pines and declaring my decision a mistake, reversing myself I drove to Sea Bright instead, a town and beach I had visited every year on my birthday since I was seventeen and could drive. I would arrive there at dawn and walk the beach, begin the next year of my life, then go to school or work. Now, as I stood next to the seawall, it was just cold, the town itself was rebuilding after the devastation left by Sandy. The bar where Bonnie and our friends had celebrated rites of spring every year, was gone, washed away. I leaned against the seawall and swiveled my head to take in the ocean, the beach, then behind me the town itself in various stages of disarray and repair. A rat scampered out from between the huge lunks of stone and brushed against my leg. That was the sign, I guessed, that it was time to head north, to dinner, my family, and a very cold Cavit Pinot Grigio.

3:15

I drove back through my home town on my way to the Parkway. I felt suddenly like a little boy again heading home after a loss at Firemen's Field. Now I was trying my damnedest to fathom what I had done.

167

5:07

Rather than drive home, I landed in Panzerrotti's parking lot an hour before rendezvous. Threefour times I pulled my phone out to call Samuelson, but I didn't. Selling the home place had been the toughest decision I had had to make prior to today. At the closing my hands shook so badly my lawyer, my lifelong friend, put his hand over mine. "Calm down," he said, "it's okay, they would understand." I got through the closing. I was happy that I had no more papers to sign.

In 1960, after Bill Mazarowski hit his seventh game, bottom-of-the-ninth homerun, barely clearing the right field wall at Forbe's field, I ran through that very house, out the back door, and leaped into the back yard. *A Cinderella season, the Pirates win the World Series!* Better still, I got to tell my father what I had seen on t.v. when he came home from work.

In an organic way the house and the family were one in my mind. Now it had all gone to smash.

The parking lot began to fill up. I numbly watched the people emerge from cars, walk hand in hand into the restaurant. Daylight faded, the temperature dropped. It was cold enough and I expected it to snow, even though none was forecast.

An hour slipped by quickly, then I saw Caitlin pull into the lot. She spotted me and pulled her car next to mine. She rolled down her window and I rolled down mine. "Hey, sailor, want to grab a drink?"

I grinned. Then Jon's car pulled up on the other side of me. "So much for the magic of the moment," I said to my wife.

"It was nice while it lasted."

"Good evening," Jon smiled, dateless.

"Where's Alexis?" I asked.

"I'll pick her up later, she thought we'd better do this alone."

"I'm impressed."

"So am I," Jon said.

6:10

We were shown to a table that looked out over the mountains. We were no frequent flyers there, but we showed up frequently enough to

168

be recognized. A server showed up quickly to take our drink orders. "A very cold Cavit Pinot Grigio," I began.

"Make mine Pinot Noir," Caitlin told her.

"What kind of IPA's do you have?"

"We just got in a Dogfish Head IPA from Delaware," she said to Jon.

"I've had it, perfect."

Silence.

"How was your day?" Caitlin asked me.

For several minutes after our wine and beer arrived we sipped and swallowed and said nothing. I had a lump in my throat and *couldn't* speak. They waited.

"I drove around after I left Samuelson at Tall Pines. I went to the house, spoke with George and Molly. Went to my old ball field, Sea Bright."

"The grand tour," Caitlin said.

"Yeah. My whole childhood packed into a few hours." I paused, the lump growing. "I want my father back," I finally said. "It's that simple. I want him back, I want the old stories, the familiarity…but I said no to the trial, the study, the experiment, to Samuelson and his drug. I'm sorry."

After a few quiet moments Jon put his hand on my arm from across the table.

"It's what I hoped you would do," he said

"Me too," Caitlin added. "His story is not the others' story. The other way might have destroyed him with kindness."

So that was that.

My father would not be part of the wake-up club. Now that I didn't have to carry the decision solely by myself, I felt lighter, the doubt from the afternoon dissipated. I still wanted my father back, of course, but in the end the risks outweighed the benefits. The right thing, in my eyes, outweighed the selfish thing.

The mood around the table lightened, group exhale, the food arrived with a second round of drinks.

"Ching ching."

"Nostrovia."

"Mozeltov."

"Remember that light at the end of the tunnel I said was the headlight on a locomotive?"

"I remember."

Jon nodded.

"I was wrong. It's not that. It's daylight—pure, simple, beautiful daylight. Let's make the best of it."

The night I proposed to Caitlin, I kissed her and looked up at the sky. "The stars seem brighter to you?" I asked her. It was corny; I knew it was corny. But it was also right. Now, at Panzerrotti's, I took a tentative first bite. I smiled, set down my silverware, and chewed.

"What?" Caitlin questioned the look on my face.

"I was just remembering the night I proposed."

"Okay."

"Well, I spoke corny but true."

"You did, I remember."

"Well tonight, for the first time in a long time, my dinner doesn't taste like ash and tough times."

"Hmmm. Not so corny."

Click.

My father parked the two-toned, blue and white, 1954 Ford near the entrance to the sand pit one Saturday morning—the same pit that we would occasionally hike to, cook breakfast on an open fire, then spend a couple of hours throwing stones at cans and bottles. But this day we were headed for the Lenape trail that wound, centuries before, from the top of Chapel Hill down to Raritan Bay, but in the nineteenth and twentieth centuries had been obliterated by the establishment of roads, houses, the cemetery, two schools—and people. So now only about a half mile of the trail still existed, and more would disappear over the next half century as the cemetery consumed more of its property for new sections and hundreds of new graves.

We walked a short way through the woods, then picked up the trail next to the ice-skating pond. We followed it to Wilson's pond, already nearly drained and sprouting saplings in my childhood. The pond, originally a hollow, or depression a few feet deep in the woods had been further excavated by my grandfather, my uncle and my father out of boredom during the Great Depression. They had squared off the edges—grave-like—and dug another few feet down and pitched shovels full, and eventually wheelbarrows full of dirt to form the banks of the pond, which was about twenty yards wide and forty yards long. It was a pretty place for picnics or to skip stones, I was told. It was never deep enough to float even a row boat or take a swim— though no Wilsons I had ever known until Bonnie and I came along ever swam, or could, because my grandfather's sister had drowned in 1916 during a Sunday School outing. Two generations of Wilsons had avoided recreational water sports.

We walked past the overgrown water hole and hiked toward what my father always claimed was a Lenni Lenape camp. That designation was based, he said, on the high number of arrowheads found in the area and especially on a large mound of dirt at the center of the camp. In addition, he and his brothers had found piles of flint and quartz chips—tell-tale leavings of flint knappers—when they were kids.

At this point in my life I was only just beginning to care much about the Lenape. I loved finding arrowheads that would wash to the surface after rain storms, but what I really enjoyed was swinging. All along the trail long sturdy vines grew down thirty or forty feet from the tops of sycamores. Mostly they tangled around limbs or the trunk at some point in their descent. My father was skilled at finding the ones that hung free, or only attached themselves in one or two places. These he would hack off a few feet above the ground, or free from the trunk with a knife or hatchet.

The vine cut free, I would hang on as my father pushed and pushed, the pendulum picking up more and more speed. I swung higher, much higher than I ever could on the schoolyard swings whose

171

ropes or chains were only six or eight feet long. A swing back and forth on them lasted maybe a second or two, a full ride on a vine lasted three or four times that long. The best rides were when, at the top of the pendulum's arc, the vine would break sending me screaming into duff and underbrush, my father and I both laughing to the point of tears.

H. A. Maxson is the author of 21 previous books, including: *Onemind: New and Selected Poems, 1976-2021; Comfort, A Novel of the Reverse Underground Railroad,* and *On the Sonnets of Robert Frost: A Critical Examination of the 37 Poems.* Nearly 2000 poems, stories, essays, reviews, interviews and articles have appeared internationally in literary periodicals, journals and anthologies as well as general-interest publications. He has been nominated for several Pushcart Prizes, and for Poet Laureate in the State of Delaware. He served as Poet-in-Residence for the Mississippi Arts Commission. Maxson holds a Ph.D. from the Center for Writers at the University of Southern Mississippi. He taught creative writing, literature, mythology and college writing for nearly five decades at the college/university level. Now retired, he and his wife, Maureen, a nurse and photographer, are organic gardeners in Milford, DE.